THE OTHER CIPHER

SOLI HANSEN MYSTERY: BOOK 2

HEIDI ELJARBO

Editor: Jill Noelle Noble

Cover design: Tim Barber, Dissect Designs

Layout: Linn Tesli

Visit https://www.heidieljarbo.com/ to read more about her books, news, events, and you can sign up for e-newsletters to hear about new releases.

"Heidi Eljarbo has certainly given herself a challenge - to write two historical periods in one novel which flow seamlessly from one to another, but the narrative works well and the two timelines inform each other beautifully...all described in sumptuous detail. If you love the art world and a good mystery, you will really enjoy this well-written book which has plenty of excitement and intrigue to keep you turning the pages...a highlight for me in descriptive writing." -Deborah Swift, author

"On its surface, this book is a wonderful mystery which will keep you guessing right up until the culprit is revealed. Underneath, this book is a story about how people can evolve and change, how different people confront challenges in different ways and how good can triumph over evil, but with a cost. If you are looking for a mystery which weaves in human themes, history and art seamlessly, please read this book." -Lynn Morrison, author

"I absolutely will be counting the days until the next one is released. I inhaled this in one sitting, it's just that good!" -Amy Bruno, Passages of the Past

"I read an advanced copy and was awed by how quickly this story and characters captured my interest. This author is one to watch! Gripping storytelling, and you won't want to put this one down till the breathtaking end." -Christina Boyd, author

"Soli is a character whom a reader can get behind and root for. I thought her depiction was absolutely fabulous, and her story drove the narrative of this book forward. Eljarbo also reminds the reader, through her portrayal of Soli, how war can consume and change the lives of ordinary citizens sometimes for the better, more often for the worse. There are several antagonists in this novel...they were masterfully drawn and wonderfully portrayed. "Of Darkness and Light" is a reward for any reader who adores quality World War II Historical Fiction. This is a book that is definitely deserving of your time. I cannot wait to get my hands on Book 2." -*Mary Anne Yarde, The Coffee Pot Book Club*

BY THE SAME AUTHOR

Catching a Witch

Trailing the Hunter

Of Darkness and Light

For our thirteen grandchildren.
Thank you for all the hugs, smiles, and sunshine.

I'm just a simple man standing alone with my old brushes, asking God for inspiration.
My passion comes from the heavens, not from earthly musings.

— PETER PAUL RUBENS

THURSDAY, 28 SEPTEMBER 1944

CHAPTER ONE
OSLO, NORWAY

THE MAN ADJUSTED the bright-red swastika armband and removed his hat as he entered the bakery. The bell above the door jingled merrily, and the aroma of freshly baked rolls, bread, and cakes pulled him inside, as if beckoning him to stay and sample a taste. Six small, wooden tables stood lined up against one wall. Each table was covered with a blue and white checkered tablecloth, and matching curtains hung in the windows. A narrow glass vase holding some kind of odd-looking flower sat in the middle of each table. The man shrugged at the feminine décor. He cared little for fripperies and flowers. In fact, he knew nothing about such things, other than presenting a bouquet to a woman could open doors.

The pastry shop was clean, and this suited him. Although it did not offer a large selection, the floors were always swept, and the chairs were in place. How he hated uneven seating arrangements and seats in disarray. Disorder was the root of downfall and prohibited progress.

The sweet-smelling pastries displayed on the shelves behind the counter may not have looked as mouth-watering had there not been a war going on. The owner probably traded flour with the Germans, as the bread seemed to have fewer potatoes than what was the norm these days.

"Good morning. You're earlier than usual," the wide-eyed waitress chirped from behind the counter.

He nodded back at her. The rosy cheeks and round mouth complemented her fair ivory skin. She'd look perfect in an ad for a healthy and happy specimen of the Arian race. But why was she unnecessarily lively? She probably slept better than he did. The dark rings under his eyes and grumpy attitude verified that. At six in the morning, he did not feel like smiling at anyone. The seagulls had been so loud during the early morning hours, he might as well have been on a ship. He glanced out the window with the word *Bakeri* written on the pane. The sun would be rising in half an hour. Not that he expected to bathe in sunlight. So far, the whole month of September had been a rainy, foggy experience. Nevertheless, soon, the streets would be teeming with people.

"Coffee?" the girl asked, tipping her head to the side. Her flaxen locks bounced on her shoulder.

"The good kind?"

"Sorry. We won't be getting any more until next week. Rations, you know. But I just made some barley coffee, and it's steaming hot."

"Well, if that's all you can offer, it'll have to do." The man placed his hat on the table by the window and threw his khaki-colored trench coat over the back of a chair. He took a seat, stretched his right leg under the table, and rubbed his knee. Wretched limb. It had given him trouble ever since he was wounded during the invasion of Norway four years earlier.

He could get better baked goods brought to his apartment than what this pastry shop had to offer, but he enjoyed the atmosphere of a quaint bakery in the heart of the capitol. Besides, his days swarmed with hard-working, ambitious people like himself, all buzzing like bees with a heavy workload. A few minutes to himself, spent watching the street through a café window as Oslo came to life, was a good way to start the day.

The waitress walked up and placed a cup and saucer on his table. She was right. Steam rose from the pitcher as she poured the barley coffee.

He watched her stroll back to the counter, her hips swaying. Alas, another customer walked in, demanding her attention.

The never-ending competition. He'd had to struggle to get to where he was in life. Education. Work. Career. Women.

He wiped the edge of the cup with a napkin before he took a slow, slurping sip.

"Weakling," people had called him in the past. "Coward."

He'd learned to make better choices, and the effort had not gone unnoticed. The respectable post at the Ministry of Communications was proof he'd come a long way from his provincial upbringing. Now, he caused women's hearts to swoon. They especially seemed to like a man in uniform. Even wearing a regular suit, he seemed to have attracted the waitress's interest. By now, the other customer had been served and had walked to the back of the shop with his cup and a plate of open-faced, goat's milk cheese sandwiches.

The man caught the waitress's eye and pulled a half-smile, and she responded by tucking strands of silken hair behind her ear. Such a pretty little thing. The apron criss-crossed in the back then tied in front around her petite waist.

"Give me my regular order," he demanded in what he perceived as a firm but friendly voice.

She responded quickly and placed a plate with two raisin buns in front of him. With a slow gesture, he put a coin in her hand, gave her a sideways glance, and winked before he closed her fist. She looked down then returned behind the counter, lifting her gaze now and again to catch him staring at her as he ate.

He finished off the first sweet then dabbed his mouth with the napkin. Enough play. He could spend hours sitting here, sipping his barley coffee, watching the waitress, perhaps ordering more baked goods. Though his palate had become more sophisticated, he would not have minded doing just that. But there were things to prepare and sort out. He picked up the cup, slurped the remaining hot drink, wrapped a napkin around the second bun, and placed it in his coat pocket. Rising from his chair, he grabbed his hat and coat, threw a couple more coins on the table, and nodded to the waitress as he left the shop.

The street outside was still quiet, with only the wind teasing a Nazi banner hanging from the second story on the building across the road. A few people rushed by, probably on their way to work. One by one, each house and building opened their window-eyes, as blackout shades were rolled up to let in the morning. A dog barked outside the butcher's shop, and the man grimaced. He'd never had patience with animals. Tiresome beasts, constantly demanding. The butcher came out, spoke to

4

the beast as if it were a person, and threw the wretched hound a bone before he returned inside. The dog wagged his tail, snatched the bone, and ran off.

Honestly, what a waste of time. But, hey, *there* was something appealing. He pulled a crooked smile. Yes, an attention-grabber like that was much better. A woman wearing a dress made of small red and white checked cloth and a knitted cardigan hurried down the sidewalk on the other side of street. No doubt, the dress had been made from kitchen curtains. She walked with a girlish gate, and her blonde curls swayed in the breeze. Behind her came another female wearing a brown beret over her short, dark hair. She sported wide black trousers and a straight coat. Wait a minute. Her? He'd seen that woman before. What was she doing out so early? He stretched his neck as she passed by. Soon, pulling the straps of her shoulder bag tighter, she scuttled around the corner out of view.

No one could be trusted these days. Not even a beautiful creature like her. Maybe *especially* not someone like her. Women with pretty faces were unpredictable and used their cunning ways to trick gullible men. *Gullible men like me?* Yes, he'd been blinded many a time and had learned the hard way to be aware of alluring looks and sweet but poisonous words. Today, he'd like to think he was smart enough to out-trick any woman, no matter how coquettish her manner was.

The man had his suspicions about that dark-haired beauty tucked in the back of his mind. Where was she going? He had to see.

He followed in her footsteps and scurried around the next corner. There she was, farther up the hill, almost by Uranienborg Church. She crossed the road and stopped for a second on the bridge overlooking the road below. He bent over, pretending to tie his shoelaces, peeking up a couple of times to see what she was doing. Soon, she continued, going in the direction of the royal palace. She did not cross the palace park but strode with a determined gait down the quieter lanes and pathways, crossed Henrik Ibsen's Street, and continued toward Vika and the harbor.

He kept a distance, making sure she did not notice his pursuit. He was well acquainted with covert surveillance techniques. He'd been trained by the best. Some operations had gone well; others had been rather unfruitful. One thing he knew for sure, he'd never divulge his reason for following her if he was found out.

He shadowed her across the street and did not look up as he heard an approaching car. A high-pitched squeal sounded from the brakes, and he lifted his gaze to see a pale-gray Opel come to an abrupt stop.

The driver rolled down the window and stuck his head out. "Watch where you're going."

"You idiot!" the man yelled back.

His mother would never have approved of such outbursts, but he was tougher now. He banged a flat palm on the hood of the car. The driver mumbled as he rolled the window back up and continued down the road.

The man looked up, glancing in the direction he'd last seen the woman. Where had she gone? He hastened his pace down toward Vika, frantically keeping an eye out left and right at every cross street and narrow passageway.

"Argh!" He kicked a lamp post then pulled off his hat and slapped it against his thigh. He'd lost her! People passing on the sidewalk turned and looked at him. He could not jeopardize his position, could not draw attention to himself with an unfortunate incident like this. He replaced his hat and tipped it to the right angle. The pursuit was over...for now.

Had she noticed? Was she on to him? He rubbed his aching leg, growled low, then marched in the direction of his office, not looking back.

CHAPTER TWO

SOLI HUGGED HERSELF as she stood in the art shop, watching the street through the large front window. Puddles glistened in the light from a streetlamp, and occasional drops of rain stirred the calm reflection, forming a multitude of expanding rings. A car drove by, and spurts of splashing water muddled the whole scene. Soli was no artist but could see ideas for paintings everywhere. Observing art was what she did. Observe and enjoy. The thrill she received from examining and learning about a painting was hard to explain. Her love of art had started when she was a little girl. She had found a book with photographs of renaissance and baroque artwork at the library. Her world had changed that day, and her mission in life had become a quest for knowledge and understanding of art history.

A man stopped in front of her window, lifted his gaze toward the darkened clouds, and shoved an umbrella under his arm before he continued. Maybe today the rain would let up long enough for her to run some errands without getting wet. Hopefully, October would prove better and show off the golden glow of autumn.

She stretched her neck. The seagulls picked scraps off the pavement outside the fishmonger's store across the road, bickering and struggling to get the last bits and pieces. They were noisy creatures, especially on mornings when Soli wanted to sleep in.

"Patience. Did your parents not teach you to be polite and wait your turn?" she said and straightened the corners of the backdrop material in the shop window.

The birds continued, flapping their wings and squawking at each other.

She had recently changed the window display to reflect the season. Pieces of framework, a couple of pen-and-ink drawings, and some art books were arranged between clusters of hazelnuts clinging to small branches on a moss-green piece of velvet. Autumn foliage was scattered about the scene, randomly yet with precision. She had shuffled through fallen leaves in the park down the street, kicking them about, thinking how pretty they would look in the retail window. Analogous colors blended the leaves from bright red rowan, to maple blades in hues of red-orange, mustard, and brown. Dainty yellow birch leaflets gave a cheerful appearance amidst the warm, deep colors of fall. She had borrowed a purple umbrella from Aunt Sigrid, fastened it to a string, and hung it wide open from a hook in the ceiling. The umbrella hovered above the exhibition as if it protected the display from the many rainfalls. Most of all, Soli hoped the complementary purple color would catch the attention of anyone who passed by on the sidewalk outside.

Given the wartime situation, her shop was doing well. *Her shop.* The thought made her smile. Now and then, she

still reminded herself that this art store belonged to her...
a woman. She kept her former employer's name on the
sign outside for two reasons. First, the store's respectable
reputation mattered in the fine art community. Though
small, Holm's Fine Art Shop was well known—even
beyond the Norwegian borders—for quality and excellent
customer service. Second, the old man had bequeathed his
life's work to her, a young woman in her early twenties.
The thought had given Soli her fair share of sleepless
nights. Why had Mr. Holm selected her as his successor in
his will? There was much to say about the man and his
choices in life. Now that he'd passed, she wished she
could ask him why he'd wanted her to continue his legacy.

Soli rolled her shoulders back. No need to keep
pondering. She appreciated the opportunity to continue
doing the work she loved. Her childhood dream of
working with art and learning about artists throughout
the centuries had come true. She gave her best and earned
enough each week to pay the rent and eat a proper meal a
day. What a blessing that was. And if she could manage to
raise the shop's reputation to an even higher level, she
would—

A knock on the back door seized her away from her
reveries. She recognized the double knock, done twice in
succession, and glanced at the clock on the wall. Only
Heddy or one of the other members of the covert art club
would come knocking two hours before the shop opened.
Soli turned her back on the window display and walked
through the front room. The walls were covered with
paintings, lithographs, and drawings. She knew each one
and had studied their histories, learned about the artists,
and had even framed many of the pieces herself. She
passed the small office on the right and the door to the

basement on the opposite side. Straight ahead was the workroom with access to the back lane and a small garden.

The knocks came again.

Soli grabbed her light-blue robe from the floor and hurried to the back door. "I'm coming." She turned the key and opened the door wide. "Good morning, Heddy. You're out before the town wakes up as usual."

Her friend looked strikingly beautiful even in the early morning hours. Heddy's eyes were like coal, and her full lips were touched up with a deep-red lipstick. Her high cheekbones gave her an emboldened look under the tilt of a brown beret.

"I need to be early if I want to come see you." Heddy folded her coat across the back of a chair then removed her beret. Her chin-length hair matched the color of her dark eyes. She plunged down on the couch Soli had slept on and stroked the sofa cushions. "This is new. When did you get it?"

"Since I left my aunt and uncle's apartment and moved into the shop, my bed has been a quilt on the floor. Nikolai brought this by a couple of days ago. Apparently, someone was selling it for a good price." Soli sank into the cushions next to Heddy and bounced up and down. "It's comfy, isn't it? And better than sleeping on hard wooden planks."

"And warmer, too," Heddy said with a grin. She picked up a bra that peeked out from between the cushions and held it up in front of Soli.

Soli giggled. "So, I'm not very tidy."

She caught Heddy scanning the room.

"No, no," Soli protested. "Don't do that. The total confusion of this room is embarrassing. I don't know why

I'm so untidy. Please pretend you don't see the mess." She snatched the bra out of Heddy's hand and stuffed it under her pillow.

Fortunately, Heddy changed the subject. "How's Nikolai doing?"

"Our friend is busy being the clever detective he is. It's been pleasant having a breather after the struggles we had last month. I mean, becoming a part of your resistance effort, pretending to be dauntless during clandestine operations—who would have thought? I don't know how I dared. I'm not as brave as you and the boys are."

"You're considerably braver than you believe." Heddy leaned back and sighed. "Besides, we do what is necessary. It's like jumping into icy water. Your body feels numb, totally insensitive to outer friction, but your brain startles and hurls you into a crystal-clear train of thought. What do I do now? How do I get out of here? What are my options?"

Soli pulled her feet up and hugged her legs. "You make it sound easy."

"It's not." Heddy gave her a lopsided smile then straightened up. "Now that you're a member of our group, there's never time to slacken in your effort or let down your guard. There is too much at stake, and we all have to get in the act and play our part. The Nazis have not stopped looting and stealing art, so we cannot quit doing what we can to preserve and protect precious objects. These items don't belong to Hitler and the German Reich."

The Art Club had recruited Soli because she had immense knowledge of art. Over the last few weeks, she and Heddy had gotten close. Even though her friend seemed fearless and determined, always concerned with the welfare of others, and her mind continually plotting new secret plans, Soli could always tell when something was wrong. She put her hand on Heddy's arm. "What's happened? You have that troubled face."

Heddy lifted her eyebrows. "More worried and serious than usual?"

Soli nodded. "Tell me what's wrong."

"Someone followed me today." Heddy leaned back again on the couch. "But he never saw me turn down your lane. I'm certain of it."

Soli sighed. "Oh, good. You had me worried there. Did you see who it was?"

"No." Heddy pushed strands of hair behind her ears. "I didn't want to appear even more suspicious to him and only got a few quick glances in his direction. I believe he lost sight of me several streets from here."

"What did he look like?"

"Knee-length coat, hat, medium height, slim."

Soli rolled her eyes, and Heddy smiled.

"I know…" Heddy laughed. "I just described half the men in Oslo."

"Not quite, and it's a start. Anything else?"

"One more thing. He had some sort of limp but walked with a firm gate, long steps."

"Well, that's something."

Heddy tipped her head. "Do you need to write this down?"

Soli shook her head. "Not really."

"You and your amazing memory." She rolled her eyes and smiled. "But for the rest of us mortals in the group, you should make some notes."

"Of course." Soli got up. "I'm making breakfast. Do you want some oatmeal porridge?"

"No, thank you. I need to run. The town is waking up now, and I have to prepare some things for tonight." Heddy arose and grabbed her coat. She smoothed down her hair, pulled the brown beret onto her head, and tipped the hat to an angle toward the left side. "Oh, I almost forgot. The reason I came by was to invite you to come along and meet some special people in one of our other covert groups. Can I meet you by the church on the opposite side of the crypt at seven?"

Soli thought for a moment then nodded. "No problem. I can be there."

"Good. I'll see you then. Oh, and, Soli, you need to use your codename there." Heddy walked out the back door and disappeared into the lane next to the shop.

Soli had used her resistance name once before when she'd met Thor Hammer, a brave and irresistibly handsome member of Milorg, the military resistance organization. She was proud of the work those "boys in the woods" did. And in the few hours she'd spent with Thor and his men, he'd charmed her down to her boots. But then, what? She'd written him—and written his family—carefully disguising any compromising reasons why they were acquainted. No one knew if letters were opened and read before reaching the recipient. She'd thought about him often, even cried a few tears, then realized the infatuation was a useless crush, time wasted on something that could never be.

She splashed some water on her face, brushed her teeth, and slipped into a calico dress with a rounded neckline and puffed sleeves. She pulled on a pair of black socks and comfortable work shoes. Time to stop daydreaming. She had work to do and paperwork and a frame to finish for a customer before she opened the store at nine o'clock.

CHAPTER THREE

THE TOWER OF OUR Savior's Church loomed high above the tram, bicycles, and people rushing on their way home from work. Even with the modest brick walls, the entire building appeared impressive on a shrouded afternoon. To enter the elaborately engraved double doors that arched the height of two tall men would not only give a person religious gratification but a satisfactory lesson in baroque interior. Well, perhaps not everyone would notice such things, but Soli's passion for art history was far beyond that of the average Oslo citizen.

The weather had not changed, and ominous clouds foretold more rain to come. Soli could have borrowed the purple umbrella from the shop's window display but chose to wear her beige coat with the matching belt over her blue woolen dress. A maroon-colored felt cloche hat matched her outfit and would protect her should the skies open.

She found Heddy behind the oak trees to the left of the church.

"I like your hat," Heddy said. "It brings out the golden glow in your brown hair."

"Thank you. Another item I inherited from my mother when she passed at the beginning of the war."

Heddy sighed. "If we'd only had our mothers longer, they could have taught us many more things we need to know."

Soli nodded. "I could certainly use more of Mor's advice."

Heddy hooked her arm around Soli's. "Are you ready to go? I said we'd be there by seven thirty."

"Go where?"

"Come, I'll tell you on the way."

As they crossed the street, Soli turned her head. The entrance to the crypt, where she'd first met Heddy's resistance group a couple of months earlier, was on the opposite side of the church. That they called themselves *The Art Club* had intrigued her. Little had Soli known then what she'd be up against. The danger of protecting and securing valuable art from a powerful enemy that had invaded her beautiful country frightened her.

Just weeks earlier, Soli had removed the antique frame from a precious portrait. She'd hidden the frame inside one of the sarcophagi in the crypt and fled the city with the painting in the middle of the night. The portrait was safe for now, but the frame was still in the crypt. How she longed to sneak down the stairs, push the stone lid of the tomb aside, and stroke her hand across the old wooden framework. She sighed. That would have to wait until her country was safe from Nazi art predators. And that day would come. Her country and people were suffering at the hands of a ruthless and greedy enemy. But she had to believe in a future as a free people again.

Heddy pulled her along. "I know what you're thinking, Soli, but we can't hold our meetings in the crypt anymore. Not after the raid last month. I've slipped inside a couple of times to check on things we've hidden there. They're still safe among the stone caskets."

"I hope—"

"I know... Your love for art will triumph, and one day, this wretched war will end. In the meantime, we'll do what we can to survive in our mysterious world of art preservation. Now, I will introduce you to even more mysteries."

Working to keep the Germans from getting their hands on artwork was an intriguing way to thwart the enemy, even though Soli's involvement with the Oslo underground filled her with unmeasurable anxiety. Going up against the occupying forces, even clandestinely, was no game, and she was painfully aware of the danger she and even some of her loved ones faced. Her brother, Sverre, had fled the country and was now waiting for further instructions in Sweden. How was he coping? Had he recovered from the abuse he'd received at the hands of the enemy? Thank God for men like Detective Nikolai Lange who'd helped the resistance members more than once. Soli had made a choice to join the resistance, and no matter how timid and terrified that decision made her feel, she would not go back to her former ignorant and indifferent state. She could not.

They passed the *Glass Magazine*, the oldest department store in town. Soli glanced at the window displays as they walked by. Their decorators did a fine job of implementing simplicity with eye-catching arrangements.

They cut across the market square, dodging vendors who were busy cleaning up after the day's work. The starving people of the capitol had purchased or traded most of the goods. Surprisingly, a little food remained; a half-full basket of rosehips, a handful or two of chanterelles, and about a liter of lingonberries—all picked in the forest on the outskirts of Oslo.

Soli would have loved some fresh produce but had not brought any money or food stamps. Her mouth watered just thinking about chanterelles fried in the pan with butter, stirred lingonberries on the side. She sighed and walked on. Maybe another day.

A sturdy woman threw water out of a bucket as they passed. The cool breeze flapped the ends of her kerchief, and wires of grizzled hair escaped the scarf on her head.

Soli jumped sideways to avoid getting the spills on her shoes.

"Sorry, miss. I didn't see you coming," the woman cried out. She wore a pair of men's boots, and a wide calico apron covered the front of her coat.

"No problem." Soli waved over her shoulder and hurried to catch up with Heddy.

"Good thing you're quick." Heddy turned her head and smiled.

"That woman looked worn out," Soli said. "She probably has more work after she leaves the market today."

Women washed clothes for the German soldiers, ironed their shirts, and mended clothing. Poverty and low wages forced women to take on more than one job. Too many had husbands who drank away the few coins they'd earned working on the dock or in factories, even before they'd returned home for the day.

Soli and Heddy walked the back roads. Up ahead, a group of German soldiers started down their side of the street. Heddy pushed Soli into the gateway of an apartment building. They hid against the wall behind the door, waiting for the men to pass. There was no need to walk right into a threatening situation if they could avoid it. Soli let out a sigh of relief when the soldiers had finally passed.

She peeked out. "All clear. They just turned the corner farther down."

Heddy linked her arm in Soli's. "I'm taking you to our chiffer group." She kept her voice low.

Soli kept walking but leaned in a little closer to hear. A group of young men stood in front of a shop window, and a middle-aged woman pushed her bicycle across the street. Anyone was a potential threat if they listened in and picked up scattered words and bits of information. She and Heddy could be arrested and even shot for aiding the underground. The knowledge of clandestine operations and gathering intelligence for the war resistance had to be kept within narrow boundaries.

"What's a chiffer group?" Soli asked.

"You'll understand more when we get there."

Soli was still a novice. Yes, she'd taken part in rescuing a valuable painting, had been on the run from Nazi sympathizers, and had even worked undercover in hopes of collecting vital information for their cause. Still, she felt like a painter's apprentice who had been handed a brush and a few colors of oil paints and told to paint a masterpiece. She could see herself standing with a palette of the primary colors of red, yellow, and blue, in addition to ivory, black, and white, and some raw and burnt umber. She'd agreed to swing that brush like a magic wand, weaving colors and textures across the canvas, but how? Why had she volunteered to do things when she had no clue how to succeed?

The determination in Heddy's steady stride made Soli quicken her pace. They followed the streets north and ended up outside a villa with a large garden overgrown with apple trees in need of pruning. Heddy opened the iron gate and let Soli in. The door to the basement was on the back side and down a few steps.

"Remember your codename," Heddy whispered.

Soli nodded. "No problem, but what about you? I've never heard you use anything but your real name."

"You can call me George."

Soli slapped a hand to her mouth to stifle a gasp. "No. Are you teasing me? George?"

Heddy shrugged. "Being a man raises credibility for someone in a leadership position. Although civilian women are strongly represented in the work we do, society in general focuses on men. I'm proud of our ladies; they keep a low profile and don't brag about the effort they put in." She grabbed Soli's shoulder. "Women like you, brave and caring."

Soli lowered her eyes and touched her warm cheeks. "Thank you," she said quietly, keeping her face averted so Heddy wouldn't notice her embarrassment.

Whenever Soli spent time with her friend, her mind opened like the parting of the Red Sea and paved the way to a new mode of thinking—a new approach of being. Heddy spoke with conviction and always had a clear target. She was a true leader, and no man could have done a better job running the art division of the resistance.

The pattern for responsibilities of men and women was set. History was proof of that. Had she witnessed any exceptions? When it came to identity, traditions were ingrained, not presumed. Not only in gender roles in society but in the everyday household chores and in professional work. Heddy's faith in the value of women in the resistance was contagious. And now, having Heddy mention Soli in the same sentence as other women who gave everything for their country, well, how was she to react? Her respect for them grew with every day the war proceeded. She closed her eyes for a moment. Here she was with Heddy. They were doing the same thing as those other courageous women. Soli did not feel brave or gutsy, but these things had to be done.

Heddy knocked on the door, and a window opened on the floor above. She looked up. "The boat has a red sail," she said, voice low.

A young man with wide blue eyes and strawberry-blond hair that fell across his left eye opened the door. "Good evening. I'm Felix. Z's expecting you."

CHAPTER FOUR

SOLI AND HEDDY followed Felix down a dark corridor and into a spacious room filled with light. Black material was nailed to the wall and covered the basement windows, and stacks of papers and a typewriter sat on a table to the left. Another table had a strange charcoal-colored metal machine that caught Soli's attention. The top lid was open, ready for use, and strips of paper spewed out, piling up, even flowing down onto the floor. Felix took a seat by the mechanism and started going through the long, narrow paper slips.

A woman with curly red hair cut just below the earlobes, squatted in the corner next to a petite girl and a somewhat taller boy. The children had the same type of hair as the woman and looked like they were about the same age as Soli's two young cousins who were seven and nine years old.

"What's she doing?" Soli whispered.

Heddy pulled Soli's arm. "Come, I'll let her tell you."

The woman was stuffing papers into the children's

oversized boots. She gazed up as they approached. "Hello, George. This must be your friend Elsie Vik. They call me Z." She stood and energetically shook Soli's hand. "I've heard about you. Only quality things, mind you."

"Well, that's a relief," Soli said and smiled. "What are you doing?"

Z winked at Heddy. "Asking questions already. That's good." She grabbed another pile of what looked like news bulletins and stuffed a few more into the children's footwear, then opened their coats and filled the pockets sewn onto the lining.

"These are my children," Z said. "You don't need to know their names."

Soli gave her a quick nod. "Of course."

Z continued fitting as many bulletins as possible into the pockets while she spoke. "We just typed and printed this newsletter. The children help deliver them on their way home."

"Illegal newspapers? But they are only children." A lightning bolt of shock went through Soli's body.

Soli's two young cousins amused themselves by writing a secret bulletin about the people in their apartment building, one they only showed to Soli and no one else. The girls were observant and sharp-eyed, picking up every tidbit of odd things. The mere thought of having them carry illegal news was terrifying. People who printed and distributed such documents could be condemned to death or be sent out of the country to Heaven knew where. How did Z dare involve her own children? A feeling in Soli's gut screamed no. *Don't send those youngsters out there.*

Z must have noticed her worry. "They are less likely to be suspected of any type of resistance work. These two

23

have been doing this for months already and know the drill." She handed the children their small backpacks and glanced at Soli. "Don't worry; they contain only school-books and pencils. See, no one will know. I'll be right back after I follow them to the door and give some last instructions."

The children disappeared into the dark hallway, and Soli's heart thumped. What might happen to them once they were out on the street?

"It looks frightening, almost like Z's ill-using her son and daughter," Heddy said.

Soli frowned. "That's my impression. They should use muscular men who can defend themselves."

"You'd be surprised to learn who the couriers are," Heddy said. "Old grandmothers out to run charity errands carry illegal news under eggs and bread in their baskets. Young women strolling their babies hide the papers under their little ones. Pregnant women tuck them under their clothes. It's amazing how inventive people are when they really want to help."

Soli's mind boggled. How could normal, untrained people gamble with their lives like that?

"But some of them get caught? I mean, there must be many involved. Those who write and print the newsletters are also at risk."

Heddy nodded. "Yes, but they're willing to take the risk and face the threat of being exposed. We do all we can to avoid fatal confrontations."

Soli was all in, totally committed to doing her part. Still, fear seemed to own her, and she did not like this part. She'd watched the children hug their mother, sweet smiles and innocent eyes wreathed by heads full of soft red curls. Soli turned to Heddy. "I know every detail is planned and prepared, but how can I get rid of the dreadful feeling that something will go wrong?"

Heddy sighed. "You can't. But you go through with an assignment, you give your utmost, then when you arrive at the next bend, you do it again." Heddy put her arm around Soli's shoulder. "Come on, girl. That's anxiety speaking. You're not one who gives up. I've seen you muster more courage and willpower than most. Yes, there are many brave men, women, and even children who defy all reason and gamble with their lives to help our effort. But remember, you can turn around any time. If you don't want to—"

"No. I want to help. You believed my knowledge of art history could be useful, and the choice was mine to make."

"Not only your knowledge, Soli. Once we considered approaching you, your brother gave a rather convincing speech about your personality and perseverance. Mind you, at first, he tried to talk us out of it. He didn't want his little sister drawn into anything dangerous."

"He's always been protective and kind."

Z returned in time for the last comment. "Who are we talking about?"

"My brother," Soli said.

"Good man." Resting her hands on her hips, Z gave Soli a determined look. "Now, what did you need help with?"

Heddy answered first. "I'd like you to show Elsie how the machine functions and what you can do with it. Your work here goes hand in hand with ours." She nudged Soli. "This team solves mind-crunching conundrums."

Z marched steadfastly to the table where the young man was punching tabs on the black machine. "Come over here and pull up a chair. I'll explain while Felix works."

Soli and Heddy grabbed a stool each and sat down. Felix focused his attention on the machine as it spit out long strips of paper, picking up random pieces and examining them periodically. How confusing and illogical it looked. Still, the people who worked here had to be far above the average thinkers.

Z put her hand on the machine. "We deal with high-level riddles and enigmas and do our best to obscure secrets from the enemy."

Felix seemed to be engrossed in his work, in a pensive place where his senses concentrated only on the task at hand. The house could probably burn down around him, and he'd not smell the smoke, feel the warmth, or hear the roaring flames.

"Cryptography has been around for a long time. Secret messages have been sent and received for as long as we've had disputes and intrigues between countries." Z's eyes lit up as she spoke, and she used dramatic hand movements to emphasize the meaning and importance of her words. "Even Julius Caesar contacted his generals by using a code merely moving every letter in his message a certain number forward in the alphabet. It sounds simple but probably took the enemy a while before they figured out what was written. In war, cryptography can give us a head start and save time."

"And save lives," Soli said.

Z nodded. "Yes, lives. That's the most important reason." She turned to Heddy. "I like this girl. She thinks with her heart, as well as her brain."

Perhaps Soli used different words than the mathematical geniuses. It did not matter. She had to be herself and do her part to the best of her ability. Z seemed to acknowledge Soli's awkwardness and continued the tour of the office.

The intriguing metal machine was next. Definitely not a regular typewriter... It had to be some sort of spy instrument, although, Soli had no idea how it functioned.

Z put her hand on the device. "This is our mechanical cipher machine, the Hagelin C-446, produced in Sweden. We call it a chiffer machine because it works with figures and numbers. This is the first thing we'll grab, should we ever have to run at a minute's notice. We even have a case for it."

A small suitcase sat under the table, open and ready to go.

"We're lucky to have one of them here in our office," Z said. "We operate with this lever on the right side. If we want to send an encrypted dispatch to our allies or fellow resistance workers, we feed the communication into the Hagelin, and voilà—they receive the message looking like these cipher texts."

"What are these?" Soli pointed to the six wheels centered on the front part of the machine.

"Cipher wheels. See how each wheel has letters in alphabetical order? If you turn each one to a specific letter, it establishes the code and encrypts the dispatch."

Good heavens. Organized secret codes? The type of thing found in an exciting novel about moles, infiltrators, and high treason? Except this was the real thing. They were living the spy story.

"Tell Soli how you decipher the encrypted messages," Heddy said.

Z pointed to two paper strips on the left side of the

device. "Those function as a double printer; one has the coded cipher text, and the other is plain, readable script.

The table was already full of narrow pieces of paper with undecipherable writing. One message was marked with red, blue, and black pencils. Z picked it up. "We received this earlier today. Felix is working on it. With the correct key to deciphering, we can feed the jumbled note into our machine to make it readable. Without a key, untangling the code can take a while."

Heddy patted Z on the shoulder. "This lady and her team are doing a crucial job for the war effort."

Z sighed. "The Germans, on the other hand, are doing the same. It's a war within the war." She kneaded her hands. "Now, who would like a cup of tea?"

Heddy stood. "Let me do it. Do you want some, Soli?"

"Yes, please."

Soli rubbed her arms. A warm drink would be perfect. The room had a humid chill, and the wood-burning stove in the corner was empty. Z needed someone to get some wood from the forest before winter set in.

Felix kept going through the strips of paper, holding them close, squinting, then frowning.

Soli touched his shoulder. "We're having some tea. How about you?"

He looked up, his eyes carrying a distant look. "No, thank you. I need to leave. I have an errand to run, and my mother doesn't want me home late." He grabbed his jacket and sixpence. "Bye, Z. I'll be back in a couple of days."

"All right, Felix. Take care of yourself."

Heddy brought the tray. Steam rose from the ceramic mugs filled with a green-herb brew. *Hmm, peppermint.* Soli closed her eyes as the sweet whiff soundlessly surrounded her. Thoughts of her mother arose, the kind of happy memories that often sustained her during troubled times. Now, here in a basement room with spy machines and the calamities of wartime both inside and outside the walls of the building, she felt peace. If only for a minute or two. All because of a sudden memory, a déjà vu triggered by the smell of peppermint.

Heddy's voice brought Soli out of her reverie.

"How do you recruit someone to come here? From what I see, they need to be able to learn and understand the theory behind this system, be clever with solving puzzles, and not be afraid to risk their life in process. That eliminates most of the people in our country."

Z swallowed a big gulp of tea. "We need number theorists, people with a head for facts and figures. Most of them are intellectuals. They're not always brave, but they believe in what we do. These are men and women who rub their hands in excitement when given a difficult riddle to unscramble."

Soli blew on the steam and slowly sipped her tea, holding the cup with both hands for warmth.

"It doesn't matter if they're young or old," Z said. "I've recently started introducing my son to the work we do here. He's particularly interested in mathematics and understands how these systems function."

Heddy widened her eyes. "My goodness. Impressive. He sounds like your son, Z."

"Well, we share that interest. My daughter sits in the corner and plays with her rag doll while her brother tries to save the world. When I bring my children with me, I can take care of them and help our country at the same time."

Heddy turned to Soli. "Z's husband was shot last year in a raid at a farm north of Oslo."

Soli could not help herself. Her jaw dropped. Poor family. Z and the children had lost their father and husband.

Z seemed to understand Soli's thoughts and touched her arm. "It's all right. I couldn't speak about it in the beginning. The pain of losing him was too great. But we've moved on and continue in his footsteps."

Heddy leaned forward. "What happened? I was told he was part of a team who monitored the telephone lines."

Z finished her tea and placed the cup on the table. "We started preparing for this warfare years before it happened. In 1933, Nils and I were newlyweds and helped set up wires that no one knew about. We even signed a document of confidentiality. I still have it somewhere. There were rumors of war already then, and we wanted to plan and prepare in case an enemy showed up on our doorstep. Nils kept up the work with the telephone lines while I began my training as a cryptologist under Captain R. Alfred Roscher Lund. Then last spring, Nils was away for a month, working on the upkeep of several cables. A convoy with Germans drove up the alley to the parsonage where he was staying. A haughty commandant jumped out of the vehicle, and the minister asked what they were looking for. 'Weapons! We've bad experiences when it comes to ministers and parsons,' the commandant answered. He claimed they'd found illegal newspapers, guns, and food stacked away in several churches and parsonages."

Z's voice was brittle, and she buried her face in her hands.

"You don't have to tell the rest," Heddy said.

"I want to. Sometimes, I need to remind myself why we're working as hard as we do and risking our lives." She sat up straight. "The German soldiers went through every building...the main house, the barn, the *stabbur*, the outhouse. The minister was gunned down right there on his front porch. Other shots were fired. Nils and his guys were involved. At the end of the day, only two of our men got away. The poor minister's wife was left alone at the farm with her four young children, her house looted, her pantry stripped of anything edible. The soldiers even took the animals from the barn." Z shrugged and stood.

Soli caught Heddy's stare. Staying unaffected after hearing Z's story was impossible.

Soli wiped the tears that ran down her cheeks and asked, "How did you end up meeting here? Nowhere seems safe."

Z sighed. "You're right about that. We used to meet in a church tower, then in a cottage behind the church down the street from here. But since the Germans have become aware of the clergy often helping the various resistance groups, we had to move again."

Soli nodded. How difficult it must have been to move the equipment and paperwork unseen, even on the outskirts of Oslo. Only weeks earlier, when she'd smuggled the painting out of Oslo, she'd barely been able to speak or breathe for fear the Germans would discover the treasure.

Z continued. "The intelligence we pick up here in our chiffer group allows our many partners in other resistance companies the ability to sabotage the enemy's effort even more than before. But the retaliations are just as tough on us. Only this month, the Germans performed several razzias a few hours north of here. Two hundred of our own were arrested and five were shot. Consequently, the Gestapo did a thorough inspection of the parsonage and church in that area."

Heddy put the cups back on the tray. "How often does the time they invest lead to a breakthrough in the resistance effort?"

"Not often, but small discoveries are often a step forward in the right direction and may lead to something bigger later on. I'm proud of our people. Their effort is important and valuable in our fight against the oppressors."

Soli checked her wristwatch. "I'm sorry, but it's late. We should get back before the nine o'clock curfew. Would it be all right for us to return tomorrow? I would like to learn more about what you do here." She turned her head to Heddy. "Do you have time to come with me?"

Heddy linked her arm through Soli's. "Of course. I have lots to learn, too."

Z smiled. "Great. I need all the support I can get."

FRIDAY, 29 SEPTEMBER 1944

CHAPTER FIVE

SOLI AND HEDDY returned to the chiffer club after work the next day. But not long after they'd arrived, there was a knock on the door, and everyone in the room fell silent.

Z went down the dark corridor to the back entrance. The key was turned, and another set of footsteps accompanied her back to the chiffer room. A man in his late twenties, wearing herringbone knickerbockers with suspenders and a knitted turtleneck sweater, barged in. He carried his sixpence in his hand and fidgeted with the glasses that had slid down his nose. As he lifted his chin to speak, Soli's shoulders relaxed. She recognized that skeptical but keen glance. It was Rolf, Heddy's secondary. No surprise he was also part of the chiffer group. The man had a keen ability to catch the points, was sharp as the blade of a dagger, and had organized his fair share of undercover actions. He could be irritatingly obsessed with details and left no stones unturned.

Heddy put her hand on his arm. "What's happened?"

Rolf was breathing heavily, as if he'd been running. "I

was supposed to meet Henry Gran by the harbor a couple of hours ago. I waited, but he never came."

Z's eyes went wide. "No, it can't be true." She glanced at the empty chair where her young assistant usually sat. "Good thing Felix's not here today. Better keep this quiet until we know what's going on."

"Who is Henry Gran?" Soli whispered to Heddy.

"He's a valuable member of this group, very loyal, and extremely skillful with numbers."

Touching Heddy's shoulder, Rolf said low, "I know it's a risk, but I should go by Henry Gran's apartment in the old part of town. I don't want to compromise his anonymity by showing up where he lives, but I have to see if he's there. Why didn't he turn up earlier today?"

Heddy gave him a quick nod. "We'll come with you." She reached for her beret and coat and turned to Z. "This news changes our plans. I'm afraid we need to leave."

Z nodded. "I understand."

To Soli's surprise, Z wrapped her arms around Soli's shoulders, hugging her fiercely. "I've a feeling you'll be back before long."

The steps creaked as Soli, Rolf, and Heddy stole up the stairs. Paint peeled off the wall, and the wooden banister needed a good varnishing. The second landing was somewhat dim with only a single low-watt light bulb dangling from the ceiling. There were three doors. Soli touched Rolf's shoulder and pointed straight ahead to the door standing slightly ajar. He stepped forward reaching out as if to push the door open, but Heddy grabbed his arm.

"Be careful. You don't know what or who might be in there."

Rolf nodded and slowly pushed the door open. The squeaking of the hinges brought a chill to Soli's spine. What would they find inside the apartment? Was she ready to face anything and anyone? She suppressed a lengthy sigh. No, she was not ready, but she had to.

A brass safety chain dangled at the side of the doorframe. It was not broken, nor were the screws torn out of the woodwork from someone forcing their way through. If Gran had received visitors, he'd let them in voluntarily.

The narrow hallway was dark. Rolf fumbled to find the light switch, but turning it made no difference. Soli stepped farther inside and switched on a light in the living room. Stunned, she took in the interior of masculine, dark wooden furniture, a worn chesterfield sofa, and green upholstered chairs. A dining table stacked with books and papers sat to the left. But what made her speechless were the walls. Artwork large and small—oil painting, lithographs, and pen-and-ink drawings in elaborate gold frames—covered the dark-blue wallpaper. Were they original or reproductions? Henry Gran was obviously a collector but also an art connoisseur. Eager to get a closer look, she walked to the largest wall to examine the artwork but tripped over a lampshade on the floor. The room had been ransacked. The floor was strewn with papers, slashed pillows, empty boxes, and broken dishes. A bookshelf had been tipped over, and books were scattered across what appeared to be a handwoven blue-and-gray carpet under the dining room table. Soli took a closer look. There were books on art history, ancient pigment techniques, and German and Italian dictionaries.

She held up a volume about attributes and symbolism

in art. "Gran is not only interested in numbers and code breaking. Just look at the walls and these books." She gave Heddy the one in her hand. "This man is obsessed with art."

Heddy looked as if she could not suppress a smile, despite the horrid surroundings. "Sort of like you?" She winked at Soli.

"I know. But what does all this mean? Who did this? And more importantly, where's Henry Gran?"

Heddy sat down and started going through papers and notes. "You've been with the man in the chiffer group, Rolf. What are we looking for?"

Rolf picked up a couple of framed photographs off the floor and placed them on a buffet. "I understand now that I didn't know him at all." He put his hands out. "Regardless of the mess, this isn't a room you see every day. Henry Gran was recruited by Z, and I've every reason to believe he was an intelligent man, clever with deciphering."

Heddy stood and flipped through papers on the table. "If we see something interesting, should we take it, just in case the villains return?"

"Let's just take a quick glance now and have Inspector Lange come here in the morning." Rolf flattened a scrunched-up document on the table and frowned. "Hey, here's something. Come see."

Many small squares had been cut out around the page, and some spaces were torn.

"This would be something you'd place on top of a text," Soli said. "My brother used to make notes like this for me when I was little. The open spaces will reveal only the letters for a coded message."

Rolf pulled a lopsided grin. "True. Good job, Soli."

A person's residence always revealed their personality and perhaps their inner thoughts and secrets, but this was different. Why did Gran have the answer sheet to a certain code in his apartment?

"All notes and findings are kept within the chiffer club, aren't they, Rolf?" Soli asked.

"Yes, we never bring anything home, but looking at this, I think he was up to something."

Heddy looked closer. "What makes you say that?"

"He's been very secretive lately, not discussing his findings with us, acting impatient and keeping to himself more than normal."

"But the chiffer club should be a safe harbor...a place where you to vent, ask questions, or discuss your anxieties about the work, right?" Heddy flipped the page over. The backside was blank.

"You would think so. Z keeps us close to her chest, but I've noticed Gran's been particularly careful and a bit distant lately. If you agree, Heddy, you should take this to Z. Maybe she can figure out what it's meant to decode."

"Good idea." Heddy handed Soli the paper. "Can you take care of this? We need to find out what Gran was working on. It was a document like this that got Sverre into trouble. He had it in his possession when the Gestapo dragged him away."

Soli folded up the paper and put it into her pocket. She kneeled and went through the mess on the floor. Every time she heard Sverre's name, her anxiety kicked up a notch. They'd managed to free him from the claws of evil people and had smuggled him across the border to Sweden. He was safer there, but she still missed her brother and worried about him.

She wiped a tear and concentrated on the mess. The

old hardwood planks had a dull and pitted surface in dire need of refinishing, much like the frames she made at the shop. Floors and framework could be painted, but if you worked with the grain, gently sanded the surface to make the most out of the wood's structure, then the natural beauty would appear and be enhanced with oil or lacquer. Every spot and notch of these boards had a story to tell. What had that floor witnessed? What had really happened here?

"Wait, there are scuff marks on the floor over there." Soli pointed to a spot near a small, toppled-over end table.

Heddy nodded toward the hallway. "Looks like he was dragged backward that way with his heels rubbing the floor." She dropped to all fours and squinted. "No blood."

"Well, that's a relief. Still, what happened here?" Rolf asked.

A loud, shrill whistle sounded out on the street, followed by the roaring of an approaching engine. The car stopped, and the noise of boots jumping out and running up the sidewalk gave Soli the shivers. A woman screamed. It was a piercing, desperate shriek.

Heddy lifted her chin. "Shh. We should get out of here."

Rolf carefully pushed aside the edge of the blinds and peeked out.

"The Gestapo is arresting someone. A woman is clinging to a man, and they're prying her away."

Heddy touched his shoulder. "Come away from the window. We don't want them to have an excuse to come up here."

He turned and nodded. "As soon as they leave, we should go."

The screams died out, and the car's engine revved as it pulled away.

Heddy let out a long breath. "Safe for now. We'll need to talk to Nikolai. He's the only police detective I trust nowadays."

"I'll do it," Soli said. "I'll send a message to the police station tomorrow morning and ask him to meet me here after I close the art shop at one o'clock."

"Good, now let's make ourselves scarce before someone returns for more."

They closed up behind them and were about to descend the stairs when a woman in the next apartment poked her nose out of her door and looked at them with eyes wide. It was not so much a frightened stare, but a vacant one, as if too many arduous experiences had numbed her soul. She was about to shut the door when Rolf grabbed the handle.

"Please, there's no need for alarm. May we ask you a question?"

The woman nodded.

"Have you seen your neighbor Henry Gran today?" Rolf spoke low, but his tone was friendly.

She kept staring.

Rolf touched her arm, and the woman suddenly focused, as if awakened from a trance. She nodded but then shook her head.

Rolf narrowed his brow. "Did you see him? It's important. Anything would help us."

She pressed the palms of her hands against her temples. "There were sounds of glass breaking, and scuffling, and—"

"When was this?"

"In the middle of the day. I didn't look at the time but

hid under my covers." She chewed her thumbnail. "I didn't see Herr Gran. Not anyone."

Rolf nodded to the woman. "Go back inside and keep your door locked at all times."

She skulked back into her apartment.

Rolf turned to Heddy. "I'll walk with you girls a distance. I don't want you two alone on the streets this late."

Heddy sighed. "But Rolf, you know—"

"No buts. I know I'm not as strong as our friend, Arvid, but I have these." He put up his fists and grinned.

"All right. We love it when you're being gallant. Come on, let's go."

Back outside, they headed up the street toward the train station, Rolf in the middle. The evening air was chill and damp. Soli closed the top button on her coat and tightened the belt.

"Rolf, you spend more time at the chiffer group than I do," Heddy said. "There was a young man there yesterday, one I hadn't seen before. Felix."

"He started a few weeks ago. I don't know him personally. Z recruits the people, and I help out when they need me." He narrowed his eyes. "Why? You seem worried."

"He's very young and reminded me of someone." She let out an exasperated sigh. "Oh, I'm tired of being suspicious of everything and everyone. Will we ever lead normal lives again?"

He placed his arm around her shoulder. "Absolutely. We'll beat this evil. One day, Heddy."

Rolf walked with them until they reached the market square, said goodbye, then headed off again in the opposite direction.

Soli leaned in and said in a whisper, "When you talked

41

about Sverre back there, I noticed the pain in your eyes. You must miss my brother, too."

A shadow of dejection swept across Heddy's lovely face. "I keep busy and try not to think about him and me. It's a good plan, but I see him everywhere." She straightened her beret. "At least, I know he's safer in Stockholm than he would be here. The Swedish government has maintained their neutrality during the war, and Sverre's commitment to the resistance effort continues in the military office there for now."

"Well, hopefully, he'll be able to return soon." Soli hugged Heddy. "We've kept a low profile so as not to draw attention to our work lately. But seeing the cipher machine yesterday made me realize how imperative it is to continue what we started. I'll be away this weekend. I leave tomorrow afternoon after work."

"Where are you going?"

Soli put a hand on Heddy's arm. "The less you know, the better. I'll fill you in later."

"Now you're the secretive one." Heddy smiled broadly. "I must have trained you well."

"You're an excellent undercover teacher, but I'm serious about this. For now, I must be cautious. But I promise, you'll find out soon enough."

SATURDAY, 30 SEPTEMBER 1944

CHAPTER SIX

SOLI PAID A young boy to deliver a message to Nikolai at the police headquarters at Moller Street 19. She closed the shop at one o'clock and walked to Gran's apartment. Under some trees at the end of the street she located a good place to wait for Nikolai. As soon as he rounded the corner farther down, she walked slowly toward him. She'd thought about him all morning, wondering how he was doing and looking forward to seeing him again.

They found the main door, walked up the stairs, and entered the apartment.

"Oh, my, they sure left a mess," Nikolai said. "Well, let's see if we can make any sense out of this." He left the blackout blinds down and turned on all the lights. Dirty dishes sat in the sink, a couple of glasses and other dishes were on the table amid all the papers, pencils, and sketchpads.

Soli picked up an open suitcase full of papers and flipped through the documents and notebooks. Some notes were coded in brief sentences, while others were longer paragraphs made up of inscrutable text. "It may not be what we are looking for, but these notes are definitely about art."

He looked at them. "How do you know?"

She pointed to a section of one of the texts. "Look at the numbers. Rare art terms are scribbled between sentences, number of pigments, and letters designating colors."

"You can tell all that by looking at a few numbers and letters?"

"Yes." Soli handed Nikolai the notebook for him to take a closer look.

"No way I would've grasped what you see, but if you say so." He gave it back to Soli. "From what I understand, Henry Gran is a valuable asset to Z at the chiffer group."

"He's a great help there. This is proof he's found a connection between art and codes. There's art in numbers and mathematics, and there's geometry in art with circles, axes, linear perspective, anything, really. Take Leonardo da Vinci as an example. His ideas about mathematics in art gained attention even in his own time, and you can see he uses his mathematical skills in paintings like Mona Lisa and the Last Supper."

Nikolai folded his arms and gazed at Soli. The well-known boyish charm of his stare all but made her topple over, but she had to concentrate. She was too engrossed in the thought of Renaissance art to get tilted off course. Not right now.

She put the notebook down and used her hands to gesticulate as she spoke. "Da Vinci proportioned the head into geometric sections, and we can divide Mona Lisa's face into rectangles and triangles and..."

She formed her fingers into different shapes, but Nikolai gently took hold of her hands and smiled.

"Let's focus on the documents," he said.

Soli lowered her eyes. "I'm sorry. I get carried away when it comes to art."

"I know, and it's amazing, really. We just need to concentrate on this now."

Did she dare ask him to bring the suitcase out of the apartment? She needed more time to go through all those documents. Hopefully, she could find out what the old man had been working on. Before she had the chance to mention it, Nikolai picked up the bag and set it by the door. "We'll bring this along. I'll drive you home after we're done here and leave the bag with you. I need you to see if there's anything in there that makes enough sense to give us some clues to what he was up to and why he's missing."

Photographs of the same man with different people were gathered on a buffet by the window. Nikolai grabbed one.

"Soli, come take a look at this." Nikolai handed Soli a photograph. The image depicted two men, smiling as they stared into the camera. "That one there with the gray beard and bushy eyebrows is Henry Gran; the other man is Leon Ruber, the head of a Jewish family that was deported a while back."

"They knew each other? This could be important. Can I take this picture home?"

"Please do, if you think it can help."

She removed the photograph from the frame and tucked it away in her bag.

"Henry Gran is carrying heavy secrets." She massaged

her forehead. "We have to find him. What do you think he knows?"

Nikolai shrugged. "No idea, not yet. First, we need to figure out what happened to him."

"Good thing he's on our side."

He did not seem convinced. "The problem is what the Germans might do if they suspect Gran has knowledge of the Ruber family's art and other valuables."

Nikolai drove Soli home as promised. She hid Henry Gran's bag of notebooks in a concealed room in the basement of the art shop then walked three kilometers before she found a bus going to Klemetsrud village. Fortunately, it was a Saturday afternoon, so the bus carried mostly Norwegian workers from the dock and harbor going home for the weekend. Had the bus been filled with German soldiers, she might not have found a vacant seat and would have had to go by foot the entire way. The ride took half an hour, and then she had to walk another thirty to forty minutes up a windy dirt road, past a few farms and homesteads, before she reached her childhood home at the end of the lane where the deep forest began. Luckily, she'd make it before sunset. There were things she needed to do before dark.

She walked up the last hill and set her bag down on the ground. The familiar white wooden house with red trim looked welcoming in the late afternoon sun. Mor's vegetable garden was to the left, and straight ahead, bordering the woodland, were the small barn and outhouse. Soli stood for a moment and soaked in the safe, loving sensation of being home.

A long-legged, bushy black dog came running toward her, tail wagging, gazing at her with wide, friendly eyes.

Soli bent down and rubbed the hound's neck. "Who are you? You're a lovely dog."

She raised her head as her father came out onto the front steps.

"Hello, Far."

"Soli, my girl." He hurried forward and swept her up in the hug of a bear, shaking and squeezing her fiercely and gently at the same time.

She laughed. "Let me breathe, Far."

He released her. "Let me look at you. What are you doing living all the way in Oslo? I see you all too seldom. How are you?"

"I'm fine, Far." She patted the animal's head and gave him a good scratch behind the ears. "Whose dog is this?"

"You remember John, our neighbor on the other edge of the woods? He came by a few weeks ago. He'd heard the Germans were checking all the homesteads in the area, looking for big hounds."

"What kind of hounds?"

"You know, all the large breeds like German Shepherds, Great Danes, Elkhounds, and Rottweilers."

This one looks like a Riesenschnauzer. He's lovely.

"Yes, he's a good animal. I'm really enjoying having him here. We'll see when John wants him back. For now, Captain is better off here. Selling your dog or even putting it down before the soldiers come and take it can result in severe punishment. An owner may get three years at a house of correction or be fined up to a hundred thousand kroner from what I've heard."

"But, Far, they could come here. Have you not thought

about that?" She frowned at him. How could he help others and take all the risk?

"Nah, they came by here the week before they visited John's place. I don't think they'll be back. Too far out of the way for them to come twice. No, those brutes will have to get their dogs elsewhere."

Captain wagged his tail and kept his eyes on his new master.

"Yes, this dog keeps me company when my housekeeper is away," Far said.

"Ingrid and the baby are not here? I was looking forward to seeing them again."

"She left a few days ago. Went to visit her parents." He put his arm around Soli's shoulders. "Come on, let's go inside."

The kitchen had a small table by the window overlooking the hilly lane and the garden. There was also a counter with a sink and a stove. Behind a narrow door in the corner was a steep ladder staircase that led to the attic and a room where Soli and Sverre used to sleep growing up. The loft ceiling was too low for Far, so he slept on the couch in the living room.

Far immediately started setting the table. "I've gotten used to having someone take care of the chores. Ingrid had better not be gone too long, or I'll have to do my own cooking again."

He laughed heartily. When Mor had died the first summer of the war, he'd been completely lost, trying to live without his best friend and sweetheart. He'd managed but having Ingrid there had cheered him up.

"I baked an apple cake this morning. Would you like some?"

His eyes beamed. Apples from their own garden. Wheat from a neighbor. What a delicious treat.

"I'd love some."

Mother's small white plates with garlands of blue flowers sat on the embroidered tablecloth. Soli could imagine Mor sitting in the next chair, her face beaming with pride at his accomplishments, as she leaned in and said, "He loves you so much, Soli. Make sure you always let him know what he means to you."

"I've fresh milk, too," Far said. "I milked the cows at Granberg this morning."

Soli closed her eyes and leaned back in the chair. "Mmm. It's been a while since I've had milk. Fresh dairy products are hard to get with the ration cards in the city."

He passed a plate with a generously sized piece of apple cake. "I'm glad you've come to see your old father, my girl, but there's something else on your mind. Do you want to tell me about it? Is there anything I can do for you?"

Soli nodded. A few weeks earlier, she'd asked Far to safekeep an item for her, something of great worth containing information that must be kept hidden from the Germans. The well-to-do Jewish Ruber family had taken care of it for generations…for centuries. Now, the unfortunate family had been deported, and their valuables were spread among greedy Nazi collectors and others who thought they could make a profit. Who knew when or if the Rubers would return? Everything was uncertain these days, and human suffering seemed to have no limits during wartime. Regard and esteem toward others were not part of the enemy's agenda.

She'd been with Heddy and Nikolai on a life-threatening mission and discovered the item only a month ago.

Her heart had skipped a beat when Nikolai had handed her the paper bag.

"I need you to take care of what's inside. Study the contents, keep it hidden, and don't let anyone know where it is. Not me. Not Heddy. It's safer if no one knows," Nikolai had said. She'd opened the pouch, and when she saw what was inside, she understood. The bag contained information regarding the Ruber family's wealth. She hadn't been able to say no. Soli had made a promise to herself, to Heddy, and to her country to fight Hitler and *the Reich*.

"Use what's in there and help us understand how to find and secure their valuables," Nikolai had told her.

"I'll do my best. I promise."

Soli sighed. Hopefully, after a better look, she'd understand how to use the knowledge. The wealthy Jewish family had collected many beautiful paintings over the years. Soli had waited for a time when she could learn about the importance of the item in the bag without being disturbed and, most of all, in a safe environment. No place was truly safe, but at the time, hiding it in her childhood home had been the best solution Soli could come up with.

Seeing the photograph of Leon Ruber in Henry Gran's apartment connected a face to the name. An overwhelming desire to help him and his family had filled her heart.

"Far, the item I asked you to keep hidden for me...I need to take a look at it."

"I wondered when you'd come back and ask about it." He pulled a small key out of his pocket and handed it to Soli. "I need to feed the chickens. Take all the time you need."

Soli trusted he had not looked inside the bag she'd

placed in his trunk, and he'd never asked about it. Respect was important to him, but he also expected it to go both ways.

He kissed her cheek then walked out the door. "Come, Captain. Let's go feed the hens."

Once her father was out of the house, Soli opened the chest in the living room. Memories seeped out as she lifted the lid, forming pictures of special events in their family's life in Soli's mind. Far's uniform from the last war, Soli's christening dress, and mother's wedding gown were on top. Soli gingerly held up the sheer white veil and stroked the lace edges. It was simple but classy. To wear this one day had been her dream since she was a little girl. She placed the clothes on the sofa and rummaged through old papers and photographs until she found the sack in the bottom of the trunk. She paused. Inside that sack was something so exhilarating, she could hardly wait to see it again. But the thrill had a horrid downside. This one item had caused a feud between the Nazis and the resistance, a skirmish that had even included a murder.

Soli folded the clothes neatly and put them back inside the trunk. With the paper bag tucked under her arm, she locked up the trunk and headed outside. The chickens were clucking cheerfully as she passed the hen house, and her father was whistling a tune she remembered from her childhood. Soli kept walking, heading for the deep woods straight ahead.

She took a detour away from the path, through moss and patches of already plucked bushes of lingonberry and blueberry. Majestic pine trees stood straight and tall, their gnarled, rose-colored branches warmed by the twilight of the sun above the horizon. Moose could be resting beneath wide branches of spruce trees, and Soli trod carefully so as not to upset any of them. A fox slipped behind a large rock, its beautiful tail brushing against a grouping of soft-purple heather before he disappeared from view.

She made her way along a winding brook, up a small hill to a spot she'd always visited when she needed to think or be alone. She sat down on a fallen tree trunk, opened the paper bag, pulled out an old ledger, and placed it on her lap.

Soli stroked the cover. Elaborate borders of leaves and geometric shapes were carved into the leather binding. The gold tooling was similar to pictures she'd seen of Italian bookbinding traditions in her art history studies. Sixteenth century, perhaps? Not any later.

The edges of the book were gilded. Over the centuries, the owners must have taken great care to preserve the metal. Only under the brass locket had the gold worn thin.

Soli pulled a pair of white ladies' gloves out of her shoulder bag. She'd worn them only once before when she'd attended her graduation ceremony. The frail pages had to be protected. She slipped her fingers into the gloves and released a long breath. What would the records tell her?

With a careful touch, she opened the old book to the first page and smiled. What a skillful calligrapher. Had he been around, she would have thanked him for his straight and precise handwriting. She'd often been frustrated trying to decipher old texts, but here, much attention had been given to the words, and the ink blotches were hardly noticeable.

Also, the ink had not faded much over the years. The calligrapher most likely used iron gall ink made from the gall nuts from oak trees. Soli smiled again. For the time being, war and misery seemed far away. She was fully immersed in art and history, her happiest place to be. She read:

Inventario degli acquisti e delle vendite del commerciante Isaac Ruber

   La Valletta, Malta, 4 dicembre 1573

She stared into space and smiled. 1573! The ledger belonged to the merchant Isaac Ruber of Valetta, Malta. This was his record of trades and purchases. Soli tapped her lips with her index finger. Malta, Malta. Where exactly was it? Ah, yes. The nation of islands off the southern tip of Italy. She'd read about baroque painters and sculptors who'd stayed there. Even Caravaggio, her favorite.

Soli had a small glossary in her pocket. She'd learned some Italian during her studies and kept the small book, thinking it might be convenient later. It had never been more useful than now. The ledger in her lap contained answers. She did not understand what or how it could be helpful at this point, but she hoped to learn.

The opening page had a pedigree chart, representing Isaac Ruber and his immediate family.

Genealogia della famiglia Ruber
Marito ~ Isaac Ruber ~ Nato nel 1548 Mantua, Italia
Moglie ~ Esther Ruber ~ Nata nel 1555 Mantua, Italia.
Morta 1593 Valetta, Italia
Figlio ~ David Ruber ~ Nato nel 1574 Palermo, Italia
Figlio ~ Yoel Ruber ~ Nato nel 1576 Palermo, Italia

Figlia ~ Fabiola Ruber ~ Nata nel 1586 Valetta, Malta

Husband, wife, sons, and a daughter. Names, birth years and places.

She smiled, and goosebumps rose on her skin as she read the youngest child's name again. *Fabiola.* Soli had come across that name in an old portrait before.

A few more names for the children's spouses and Isaac Ruber's grandchildren had been added below. A warm feeling moved through Soli. Knowing something personal about this family made the ledger even more valuable to her.

The next headline simply said, *Acquisti.* Purchases. She carefully traced her finger down the list of transactions, flipped through the fragile pages, and scanned for entries that emerged from the leaf, telling her she should look further. The likelihood that the twentieth century Ruber family still had all the items purchased in the ledger was improbable. But their descendants had certainly taken good care of many heirlooms, and Soli had seen some of their treasures at previous auctions in Oslo. She hoped to find something that had survived to her day, precious items she and her friends in the resistance could protect from Hitler and his mercenary fortune-seekers.

Concentrate. Today, her main purpose was to find out about any old and valuable pieces of art, something the Germans would trample on corpses to discover and seize for the Führer—or if they were even greedier, keep for themselves.

The Jewish merchant of old must have done well. He went into the seventeenth century, a husband and father of three during a period of empires, slavery, and great power in Europe. People traveled more, and thoughts and ideas spread across the continent. Soli closed her eyes. *Imagine what it would have been like to live in Isaac Ruber's time.* Intellectuals like astronomers Galileo Galilei and Johannes Kepler put together the puzzle of the universe. Francis Bacon and Rene Descartes enlightened people with new science and philosophies, while William Harvey mapped out the anatomy of the body. And the art! Oh, to have been there and seen her most favorite painters in action.

Purchases had been made of china, gold, enamel, and art. Without a doubt, Isaac Ruber of Malta had been a member of the privileged upper class and a solid head of a wealthy Italian *famiglia*. Was it possible to envision their lifestyle? What had Isaac Ruber been like?

Soli continued reading. Some items had been resold, but it seemed like most of the acquisitions were for Isaac Ruber's personal collection. A pair of carved wooden figures, a gilded mirror, embroidered silk, candlesticks, porcelain and ceramics, and jewelry—in fact, quite a few pieces of jewelry.

Signora Ruber must have been a most bejeweled woman. Knowing the Italians owned the Renaissance with their glamorous appearance, Soli pictured Isaac Ruber's wife—heavy silk gown with a pointed neckline, her skirts swishing as she strolled through the halls of their mansion; an embroidered collar with pleated puffs emphasizing her elegant features; fine, bow-embellished, high-heeled shoes clacking as she stepped down the stairs; perhaps a feather fan hanging from a cord around her waist.

Soli paused, her finger lingering on an entry. The handwriting had changed. A new, less elaborate script alternated with Isaac Ruber's calligraphy. The family was not in Malta anymore. She flipped the pages back and forth. Had they moved? A smaller purchase of a pair of silver candlesticks had been made in Antwerp, Belgium, a ring with rubies, gold-and-glass earrings, three meters of lace, and a vase. Then an interesting account of a dowry for a Jewish wedding.

"What about art? Why haven't they bought any art for a while?"

Soli stretched her neck and gazed toward the setting sun. Darkness would soon cover the woodland. She needed to get back to Far. She glanced back at the book. What was she looking for? Which famous painter lived in Antwerp at that time? Her mind raced, trying to find clues to an art purchase... Anything that could be connected to Leon Ruber in Oslo, a painting important enough for the Germans to be willing to go through fire and water for.

She was about to pack up and go back to the house when a record seemed to materialize on the old page.

Un pittore d'arte. A painter of fine art. And the letter R... No, she could not read the whole name. Ruber? No, that wasn't it. The rest of the word was missing. Had it been scratched out or erased?

Next to the entry, on the left margin, someone had written a number. The ink was newer and the handwriting more like that of Soli's own day. She tipped her head to read the fourteen digits.

Soli spent a few minutes directing all her energy to memorize the last entry, the genealogical page, and other interesting transactions, then she closed the book and placed it back in the paper bag. She removed the white gloves and released a long sigh. Her eidetic memory, the ability to recall an image in specific detail, would come in handy, especially now. Carrying the information in written form was not an option. She had not had time to go through everything in detail, but now the memories would appear as photographs in her mind, even when she put the ledger back in Far's trunk. The book had to stay hidden. In the hands of the wrong people, more art treasures could disappear and end up in Hitler's personal museum or hidden behind the closed doors of one of his many dishonest associates. More than that, to acquire such art, greedy men went to extreme measures.

Soli lay down on the soft moss and soaked in the last beams of sunset. *Every shore has a story.* The infinite waves, the temperamental wind, the ever-mesmerizing view to a distant horizon were all part of the narrative. *Every river has a goal.* Where was it going? When will it get there? What would it see along the way? She lifted her hand and with her index finger traced the reddish-brown tree trunk of a pine tree all the way up to where the gnarled branches twisted against the evening sky. *Every tree has a purpose.*

The ledger had a wealth of information. She only needed to understand more. Who was the fine artist, and what had Isaac Ruber bought? And what did the fourteen-digit number in the margin mean?

She hurried back to the house and hung her coat on a hook in the hallway. As she entered the kitchen, she stopped and drew in the odor wafting in the air. The aroma of meat, vegetables, and herbs bathed the room. Apart from the slice of apple cake earlier, she'd not eaten since yesterday, and her stomach clenched with hunger.

Far stood by the stove, stirring a large, cast-iron pot. "Ah, there you are, Soli. I was getting a little worried. It's dark outside now."

She stretched up and kissed his cheek. "No worries,

Far. These are my woods, remember. I could walk home blindfolded if I had to."

He just smiled and threw Captain a bone. The dog wagged his tail and ran outside.

Soli peeked into the pot. "It smells wonderful. Rabbit stew?"

"Yes, I received a rabbit as part of my payment for milking the cows this week. Go wash your hands. Supper will be ready soon."

Soli washed up then replaced the ledger while Far was busy in the kitchen. The living room was the same as it had always been. She paused for a moment by the wedding portrait of her parents on the wall. How grateful she was for good parents who wanted and loved their children. Now that Mor had passed, Soli treasured every minute with Far even more than before.

They sat down and ate together, spoke about her work and dreams, and before long, he asked the question she'd known he would ask.

"Have you heard from your brother?"

Far knew Sverre had fled to Sweden, although Soli had withheld the details regarding why.

"He's in Stockholm, Far. I've been told he's safe."

Far let out a contented sigh and bowed his head. "Good, as long as we know he's alive."

Soli stretched her arms and yawned. "I'm ready for bed. Let me help you clean up first."

But he wouldn't hear of it. "No, no. You go on. I can do it." He gave her another hug. "Sleep well, my sunshine."

Home felt safe. Soli climbed the ladder and crawled into her old bed. Spending a few hours with her father was precious time.

She opened her shoulder bag to get her handkerchief, and her fingers brushed the photograph of Henry Gran and Leon Ruber. She'd been preoccupied with the ledger in the forest, but now, she pulled out the framed picture. She held it under the light of the lamp on the nightstand. What was Mr. Ruber holding in his hand? She squinted, then her jaw dropped, and she leaned back against the wall. The ledger. Which meant Henry Gran must have seen the precious book. What did he know about the information it held? Was he acquainted with the treasures and artwork of the current Ruber family? Her mind spun with the possibilities.

With a sigh, she put the photograph back inside the bag and switched off the light. Pulling the feather-filled cover up to her chin, she lay back on the pillow. "Where are you, Henry Gran?" she whispered. She could not help wondering if the disappearance of the old man had something to do with his discoveries and now hers. Were they on the same track? Certain the numbers written in the margin was a code to a piece of artwork, she had to make sure she got ahead of the enemy before they found out.

Soli closed her eyes and drifted off to sleep, listening to Far humming downstairs. Right now, right here, the world was a safe and pleasant place to be. But who knew what danger lay ahead once she returned to Oslo?

~ CAPITOLO I ~
ANTWERP, 1613

THE AIR WAS COOLER by the garden wall behind the sienna-colored brick mansion. Fabiola sat on the marble edge of the fountain. The wind was rising. It ruffled the water's surface and formed miniature waves with foamy crests like lace edges on the sleeves of a gown.

"Come, let's go inside now," Signora Nava beckoned, her voice still feminine and soft, although the creak and hoarseness gave away her old age.

The senior lady had been a faithful chaperone since Fabiola was a young girl. Now, Signora Nava's face was crinkled and her back a little crooked, but she took her responsibilities seriously. Father was a respected merchant with much influence, but he seemed even more concerned with Fabiola's welfare. Only a trusted family friend could accompany and supervise his only daughter in her daily activities.

Fabiola did not want to leave. Not yet. Not until the clouds let go, and cool drops of rain fell to the ground, blending the scent of the floral garden with the earthy smell of soil, rocks, and grass. Not until the wind danced around her head and pulled strands of long, dark tresses away from pins and combs. The sensation of nature playing with her, touching her skin, made her feel alive.

She slid the tips of her fingers through the ripples on the water.

Signora Nava nudged her again, and with keen brown eyes she looked at Fabiola, determined yet gentle. "Come, child."

With the rain came a gust of wind that rustled the deep-blue sweet peas against the stone wall. Fabiola lifted her face to the sky, closed her eyes, and allowed the first drops of cool drizzle to touch her cheeks.

"Fabiola, you'll catch a cold."

"Yes, Nava, I'm coming... Isn't it refreshing?"

She followed her older companion up the path to the main house and into the hallway with its grand pillars and carved oak staircase that curved upstairs to the bedrooms.

Fabiola took hold of her deep-green chintz gown and hurried up the steps. Her padre imported material from India, knowing she loved the rich, natural colors. The material swooshed as she moved, and she slowed as she approached the nursery to the left at the top of the stairs. The room was bright and cheery—a buoyant contrast to the dark wood and deep wine or navy wallpapers in much of their home. When Annarosa was born three summers ago, Fabiola had engaged in long discussions with her husband, Eli, who thought every chamber of the house should portray their wealth and influence. He'd finally given in and let her decorate their daughter's nursery. She'd told the workers to leave the whitewashed brick walls and add curtains and pillows in sunny colors.

Hester, the nursemaid, sat on a chair. Fabiola nodded

to the young woman then tiptoed to Annarosa's bed. She stroked the round cheeks, rose-colored by the heat.

"You are sincerely loved," she whispered.

The little girl's auburn-colored angel locks graced the embroidered pillow, and Fabiola twirled her finger around the silken strands.

"Let me know when Annarosa awakes from her nap. I want to play with her in my room," she said low.

Hester stood and curtsied as Fabiola left the room.

Fabiola walked down the dark hallway to her room facing the street. Eli had drawn the line about having their daughter share a bed with them.

"Only the poor sleep together like a litter of kittens," he'd said.

Sometimes, Fabiola asked the nursemaid to bring Annarosa into the large canopied bed with its heavy curtains. They'd nap together amid large feather pillows and embroidered covers. Sleep was never sweeter than when she could drift off, listening to the little angel breathing.

The room had a tall lattice window overlooking the river Schelde. Fabiola sat down by the dressing table and looked out. She'd arrived in Antwerp four years earlier when her padre had brought their family—including Fabiola's two married brothers, David and Yoel—all the way from Malta. He'd combined his trading business with that of an old Italian partner and friend. It had been a wise investment. Their trade had doubled several times over, and the future looked bright for the two merchants and their families.

Looking in the mirror, she saw the reflection of a pale face with a hollow gaze. Her padre had meant well marrying her off to the son of his companion. Fabiola had never doubted her father's love; he'd meant to secure her future.

Could an arranged marriage become a happy union? Was it possible to feel her heart skip a beat, her fingertips tingle with anticipation, and her knees weaken once again? Padre had promised her a prosperous and protected life. He was pleased with his choice of a husband for his daughter. The two families were well acquainted in life, business, even in faith. To the two men, the blending of their children seemed honorable and socially accepted.

Signora Nava came into the room and pinned Fabiola's windswept locks back into place.

"There," she said. "Beautiful, as always, but why are your eyes sorrowful?"

Fabiola shrugged.

Nava started humming and added a decorative comb with pearls to Fabiola's hair, one of the gifts her husband Eli had bestowed upon her. A reminder that he cared, even though he traveled to foreign lands much of the time.

"I'm finished, child. Are you pleased with it?" Nava bent forward and stroked Fabiola's cheek. "Are you thinking about your husband again? You'll learn to love him, child."

Fabiola sighed. Her older brothers were probably right. She should not moan or complain about her situation. And it was not in her nature to whine. She'd seen others act as if courting was a game of charades. To her, it meant more... She wanted more.

Fabiola walked downstairs to the parlor. A maid curtsied and asked if she needed anything.

"Something sweet. Will you bring it here?"

Minutes later, the maid returned and placed a plate

with pie baked with sugar and spices on a small oak table. Fabiola's husband's trade resulted in exotic luxuries from across the Mediterranean, India, and even Japan and China. He returned with spices, tea, gems, and tobacco. He'd bring silk and quality materials, and their kitchen boasted the finest china. But the one thing she enjoyed above all was the sweetness of sugar from the south-west colonies.

Fabiola pushed the chair upholstered in needlepoint red cushions to face a portrait on the wall. She nestled into the seat to study the painting. She took a bite of the delicate cake. *Mmm*. The rich, spicy flavor exploded on her tongue. What a delightful treat.

She glanced up at the portrait again, and her mind wandered to the day she'd sat in the artist's studio in Valetta, Malta and had her likeness captured by a master painter. The scene brought back their conversation, laughter, and the feelings she'd developed over the course of their visits.

He'd died the year after she'd arrived in Antwerp. What a waste of a brilliant talent, of a man whose heart was good, at least in her eyes. The last time she'd seen him was five years ago. She had no free will to stay, no free agency to choose her own life. Fabiola squared her shoulders. *No, don't dwell on that.* She'd written a letter. What else could she have done? Her heart had been broken, and she could not face him to say goodbye. Her padre had left Malta and brought the family northward. They'd traveled by horse-drawn carriage to a new home, a new life. Padre was optimistic they'd be safe to practice their religion, but being a Jew was also difficult here.

They would always be Italian, and they used their own

language and kept the same customs as before. Annarosa would grow up knowing her heritage and religious roots.

The best part of Fabiola's day was the couple of hours she spent with her daughter. How could a blessing be so sweet? Alas, Eli had insisted that as a well-to-do wife of a citizen of Antwerp, her duties involved running the household and directing the servants, not taking care of children. She had pleaded with him, tried to explain the joy she experienced in spending time with their little girl, but to no avail. Though he was a good and just man, he was firm in his opinions and beliefs. Oh, to be allowed to voice her opinion, to be granted the time of day to share her sentiments.

Not once did he ask about her thoughts, her feelings, or her life before she came under his protection. And she never offered those inner contemplations. Would he consider it a misuse of his time, or would he listen?

She'd loved before, deeply and without regret. Only Nava knew about the innocent affair. What if Eli discovered Fabiola would never forget the artist who painted her portrait before they left Malta? Would it bring shame to her husband?

Fabiola walked toward the window and let out a disheartened sigh. No, Eli could never know. Could she learn to continue? Being bitter would only hurt herself. She truly desired to be grateful for the good memories and revive her life.

The clouds had dispersed, and dogs ran on the riverbank, barking and playing. People returned from the market, carrying baskets of vegetables and grain. On the road in front of the house, a man with a black felt hat walked by. He carried a canvas under his arm and a few paint brushes in his hand.

As she watched the man disappear down the sidewalk, a most intriguing notion filled Fabiola's mind. She rubbed her hands on her gown. There was much to do. She was capable of independent thought… Well, to a certain point. If she dealt with the situation in a proper and feminine way, she would no doubt find a means to attain permission to carry through with her brilliant plan.

MONDAY, 2 OCTOBER 1944

CHAPTER SEVEN

OSLO, NORWAY

IT WAS A BUSY day at Soli's shop. A woman brought three drawings and asked to have them mounted by the end of the week. A birthday present for her husband, she said. Some people still had money to buy gifts, and Soli was more than happy to make the frames herself. Another customer was an old regular. He collected expressive paintings done in a warm and colorful palette. Soli had found two floral motifs by Norwegian artist Hans Ryggen a few weeks earlier, and the customer purchased both, including the elaborate golden frames. The afternoon she spent sorting out papers in the office—an unpleasant but necessary part of business ownership.

Soli stood by her small stove in the back room. She'd been lucky to get some fresh vegetables from the grocery store on the corner. Into a pot, she'd added bouillon with a couple of potatoes, kohlrabi, leeks, and a carrot. Steam rose as she ladled the soup into a green bowl. She grabbed a spoon from the top drawer and sat down on her sofa-bed with the hot bowl in her lap and a notebook and pencil on the side.

Unanswered questions spun in her head. She could not stop thinking about Henry Gran. The old man was still missing, and she prayed he did not suffer. What had happened to him, and who had dragged him out of the apartment? What had the kidnappers been looking for? More importantly, had they found anything?

Then there was the cryptic information she'd found in the ledger. The transaction date of the unknown work of art was 1613 and had taken place in Antwerp, Belgium. The painting was so far without a title. As far as an artist was concerned, Soli only had the letter R. And what about the slew of numbers in the margin, obviously written much later? They made no sense to her, not yet. But they had to be important. Why else would they be there?

She finished her soup then put the bowl and spoon in a wash basin. She'd do the dishes later. There was no time to heat the water and clean up. She had an auction to go to.

* * *

When the gallery on Bygdoy Allée had their September auction, they invited all the town's art dealers. Soli had attended the last few years and always found it interesting. She hurried past the town hall and the harbor, up the smaller roads to Henrik Ibsen's Street, and turned left on Bygdoy Allée, known for its chestnut trees adorned with fiery autumn leaves. As she neared the gallery, she was glad to have arrived without having tripped or broken an ankle. Her new fish-skin shoes had higher heels than she was used to, and dodging the uneven cobblestones and neglected potholes in the road was no easy feat. Wanting to appear professional, she'd worn her taupe dress suit. It had a nice belt, and the pretty ruffled neckline on the white shirt underneath showed, even when the jacket was buttoned up.

She pushed her wavy hair behind her ears and walked about the crowded room, listening to the buzz of conversations and taking in the display of paintings, lithographs, and drawings.

"Elderberry cordial?" A young woman presented a tray filled with goblets of red juice.

"Yes, please." Soli helped herself to a glass and slowly sipped the drink.

Oh, the benefits of being invited to special evenings like this. She greedily inhaled a larger gulp but swallowed down the wrong pipe when she saw a tall, distinguished-looking man on his way to the exit. Stifling an upcoming cough, she tried to clear her throat and turned her back on the front door for a moment, not to gain any attention. It must have been him. Lieutenant Colonel Heinz Walter, notorious art collector, ruthless Nazi, absolute enemy of everything Soli held dear. She'd spoken with him before, even spent an evening with him. He had the kind of presence that made women unconsciously bat their eyelashes at him and men stand agape in awe and admiration. Plenty of ribbon bars covered his immaculate uniform, and he wore aiguillettes, those braided, decorative golden cords, dangling from his shoulder and impossible to miss.

She slowly turned and tilted her head. He still carried that dagger on his hip. Yes, the lieutenant colonel was an impressive man in many respects. But Soli knew better.

Heinz Walter had a dark side. He was only loyal to himself and possessed neither mercy nor conscience. He would commit murder—or order someone else to do it—if it meant getting what he wanted. She closed her eyes. The way he'd treated Sverre... She did not even want to go there. Heinz placed his visor cap on his head, clicked his heels to a man standing next to him, and strutted out the door.

It took a minute before her breathing returned to normal. With a shaking hand, she took another sip of the elderberry cordial. What was he doing in Norway? She'd heard he left for Germany, but that was about a month ago. What if he'd seen her standing there? Would he come back?

Someone touched her shoulder, and she jerked around, almost spilling the rest of her drink.

"Nikolai. You've no idea how glad I am to see a friendly face right now." She kept her voice low. "Was that—?"

He nodded. "Yes. Supposedly, he's been in Oslo a couple of days. I wonder what he's up to."

Soli leaned in. "We should find out why he's here. Last time he came, he was looking for information about hidden art just like us. Nikolai, the man is evil."

"I know. He's not someone we want to cross paths with."

Soli checked that no one stood close enough to over-hear her words then continued. "I spent Saturday evening reading through the ledger. The Ruber family had another baroque painting."

"Are you sure?"

"Yes, positive. I haven't figured out where it is yet, but seeing Heinz Walter here makes my imagination run wild.

What if Henry Gran knows something, and Walter interrogated him? What if the lieutenant colonel is after that same painting? I have to find out what it is and where it's hidden."

"Well, he's left for now. I don't think he'll return here tonight. His visits are usually short. He finds the information he needs, hands out orders, and lets others do the dirty work for him."

"He could do most of those things from his headquarters in Berlin."

"True, but it might not make any difference for us." He touched her arm and gave her a comforting smile.

Instantly, Soli grew more at ease. Nikolai always made her feel safer and calmed her when she did not know how to bridle her worries.

"Go mingle, Soli. Do what you came here for. Tomorrow, I'll snoop around at the police station and see if someone knows what he's up to this time. All I know for now is that he was talking to that man over there."

He casually tipped his head, indicating a clean-shaven, chin-up kind of man on the other side of the room. The man was adjusting the frames on the wall, making sure they were all aligned and level. Soli cringed when frames hung crooked, too, but she'd never straighten off-kilter paintings in somebody else's gallery. Apparently, this fellow could not help himself and took his time, stepping back to observe then adjusting a little more. As he moved, he dragged his right leg. Did he have some kind of injury?

"Who is he?" Soli asked.

"Sophus Bech, a newcomer in town. From what I've heard, he studied in Germany and was enrolled in the Gestapo down there. He has a post at the Ministry of

Communications in Oslo now and is supposedly a bright young man."

"German then?"

"No, Norwegian. Speaks both languages fluently."

The gallery owner walked by and asked for Nikolai's assistance.

He bowed. "Of course, I'll be right there." He turned to Soli with a concerned look. "Duty calls."

"I'll wander around the gallery with the ears of an owl. The more information we can gather about what's going on in the art community of Oslo, the better." She gave him a mischievous grin. "And I have a few items I'm interested in buying, also."

As Nikolai headed off toward one of the back halls, Soli nonchalantly scanned the room. Where was Sophus Bech now?

There, next to a wall of watercolor renditions, stood the new protégé, speaking to Mr. Lorentsen. No doubt, Sophus Bech was someone's charge, an understudy in the Nazi world, on his way up in the hierarchy. Casually, she made her way across the room. A whiff of Old Spice loitered in the air around Bech. A common aftershave, but not Soli's favorite. She stopped close enough to eavesdrop and put on a pensive look, as if she studied the charcoal drawing on an easel by the aquarelles.

"Did you hear about Henry Gran?" Mr. Lorentsen asked. He stood, legs wide apart, all protruding belly and chubby, dimpled cheeks. He was always friendly and an avid collector of modern art. He was also known as a fierce competitor among the art dealers of the city.

They both knew about Henry Gran? Soli strained to listen, not wanting to miss a single word.

Bech stood, hands on his back, and moved his chin

forward. He squinted and shook his head. "Noooo, do tell, Mr. Lorentsen."

"No one seems to have heard from him. He never misses our art appreciation meetings or discussion forums. We've had two such gatherings this weekend, but he did not show up for either of them. One of my colleagues went by his apartment, and Gran wasn't there. The neighbor woman had expressed concern, saying he was missing, and the police had been by."

"Good heavens." Bech's voice sounded dramatic, almost theatrical.

Suddenly, Mr. Lorentsen turned to Soli and stretched out his hand. "Well, good evening, Miss Hansen. We meet again. Let me introduce you to Sophus Bech. He works for the Ministry of Communications. Mr. Bech, this is Miss Soli Hansen, an excellent art historian and the owner of Mr. Holm's Art Shop."

Soli's plan had gone awry. She could not be a mere fly on the wall, an invisible bystander who listened in on the conversation without being noticed.

Bech shook her hand but said nothing. Gray, deep-set eyes stared. How uncomfortable. It was as if he communicated through a glowering, slow blinking. Soli turned her head to avoid his relentless gaze.

"What do think about these watercolors, Mr. Bech?"

He folded his white, long-fingered hands, stretched them out, and cracked the knuckles. "Why be interested in pale, water-based solutions when you can have the passionate, constant colors of oil?" He clicked his heels and left.

Soli caught Mr. Lorentsen looking her way. He started laughing.

"The man obviously knows little about the diversity of

the art world," he said. "Oh, well, he probably tries his best… Whatever that is." He held out his arm. "Come, Miss Hansen. May I accompany you to the auction in the other room?"

She accepted his arm, and they found seats on the back row in the adjacent room. In front of them were six more rows of chairs and a table where the auctioneer stood, hammer in hand, ready for bids. Two assistants stood on either side and promptly displayed the pieces for sale on the auctioneer's list.

Soli had already checked the catalogue and picked out three items. One was a fairytale drawing by Theodor Kittelsen. It was costly but would make a good investment. In a way, she hoped not to resell it and rather keep it for herself. The others were painted by a modern artist —two abstract, non-figurative pictures of life in the city. Not the style she preferred, but she could easily resell them at the shop.

At least, there were no revolutionary pieces of art that evening. No impressionistic French paintings, British Victorian, or even Art Nouveau and Modernism. The National Gallery in Oslo had hidden their art from the Nazis, as had the Louvre in Paris and other museums. The Nazis had been looting and confiscating art for years. No wonder the selection was scarce. Not that she could afford a famous work of art, but she would like to see the pieces one day without visiting Hitler's planned art museum in Austria.

One day, Soli, there will be peace, and you can travel to any country you like and visit museums, galleries. You can enter old churches and basilicas and view ancient paintings above the altars in their side chapels.

She'd never give up that dream. Not ever.

The drawing by Theodor Kittelsen was sold to someone else. The bidding spiraled beyond what she could afford. She should have known. It was the most sought-after picture that evening, at least in her eyes. The two abstract paintings became hers. The gallery assistant wrapped them in brown paper. They were small enough for her to carry under her arm.

Soli headed back to the front room. The thought of meeting Heinz Walter or even Sophus Bech out on the street sparked a fear that turned into painful lumps in her stomach. Where was Nikolai? She'd not seen him much all evening, and he'd promised to take her home.

She stood and waited, nodding and smiling to people leaving, at the same time digging her fingernails into her hand.

Suddenly, his deep, soothing voice came up from behind. "Are you ready? I'm sorry you had to wait."

"It's all right, but I'm glad you're still here. I was worried you'd been called away to some assignment."

"No, only the manager who wanted help with security in the back room." He looked at the brown paper package under her arm. "You bought something?"

"I did. They're for the shop. Hopefully, I'll sell them for a profit."

He drove her home. They spoke of good things, no war stories, no discussions about Nazis, abductions, or horror. They must have both needed a few non-eventful minutes of leisurely, uplifting conversation. The more time she spent with Nikolai, the more she came to know the man beneath the outer shell of courageous detective who'd rescued her and her friends from danger. He genuinely cared for people. If it had not been for Nikolai, her brother would probably not have been alive today.

When he stopped the car outside Soli's building, he turned to face her. Those deep-blue eyes locked on hers, and, suddenly, all she wanted to do was throw her arms around his neck. He'd been there for her, listened to her concerns, and offered good advice. Despite his incredible charm, her common sense bridled her spontaneous urge to physically thank him.

"I appreciate you driving me home, Nikolai," she said with a smile. "And I'm glad you were there when both Heinz Walter and Sophus Bech showed up."

"No problem. Those are men you should stay away from. Good night, Soli. I'll come by the shop tomorrow afternoon, and we can talk more about the missing painting."

* * *

Back inside her room at the shop, Soli put a log in the wood-burning stove and changed into her nightgown.

If Sophus Bech was chummy with the likes of Heinz Walter, he could be a poisonous, dangerous liaison. He'd not said anything enlightening; in fact, it was more what he didn't say. Bech had not reacted properly when Mr. Lorentsen spoke about Henry Gran, and Bech had been awkwardly quiet in front of Soli. No doubt, the man knew more than he revealed.

She'd greeted a few other art dealers during the evening. Some were obvious in their dealings with the Nazis. They'd made their choice and earned their money collaborating with the enemy because they did not see a future as a free country ever again. Art changed hands often enough, and she'd been part of that exchange during her time working in the art shop, going to auctions, buying and selling. But she'd noticed too often how German-friendly dealers took the finest things, confiscated, stole—whatever suited them best. Soli intended to take a more ethical tact, to be fair about the preservation of art. It was wrong to prey on people who owned valuable art, regardless of their religion or cultural background.

She got Henry Gran's bag containing the notebooks from the hidden room in the basement and sat down under the covers on her sofa-bed. She flipped through two or three sketchbooks and notepads. Soli leaned her head against the wall and sighed. She had to get someone to teach her the beginnings of cryptography. To her, Gran's notes looked like illegible scribbles. The pages seemed to have a pattern, and in each book, she recognized a few words.

PY for yellow, PR for red, and PB for blue. The long list of codes for various colors was easy to understand. Some pages had lists of color series with the highest number showing the most expensive pigment. Gran had also categorized the character of each pigment with their names. Ultramarine, Prussian, Cobalt, Cerulean were some terms for blue. Soli had experimented with pigments during her art studies. She'd painted small sections of colors and sprinkled salt into the damp paint to see how it reacted. Seldom had she met anyone as fascinated in the details of art as she was, but like herself, Henry Gran was interested in the painter's palette.

The next pages in the notebook had a glossary for Italian art terms. *Arte, pittura, pigmento, colore, bella modella, cane.* Soli recognized most of the words, such as art, painting, and color. But cane? What did that mean? She drew a quick breath. The word meant dog. Gran had written the Italian words for beautiful model and dog. Why?

She continued on to the next journal. Much smaller than the others, this notebook was written in a strange script that did not resemble normal lettering. Where had she seen writing like that before? Sleep was far away now. Staring into nothingness, she rocked back and forth, tapping her lips.

Ah, Leonardo da Vinci. She'd borrowed a book from the library during her studies, a diary written by the great Renaissance artist. Da Vinci was left-handed and wrote his notes mirror-wise. She ran and picked up the hand-held mirror on the sink and crawled back under the cover.

"You're a lefty, Henry Gran. Now, let's see what you've written."

Gran was analyzing a certain painting using codes and clarifying the application of light and dark in the composition. More certain than ever, Soli understood what type of painting she was looking for. She'd identified the pigment used, the procedure, and the structure. Every art movement and period had its own palette, its own use of dominating colors. Just like she'd read in the old ledger, Henry Gran's writings pointed toward one art period. Baroque. The painting he described could be a Caravaggio or any of the artists who'd followed him and learned the chiaroscuro technique.

The clock on the wall read after midnight. She put the bag back downstairs and got ready for bed. Just as she turned out the light and curled up into a comfortable position, there was a knock on the door. She did not dare turn on the light but waited. Two knocks, done twice in succession.

This time of night? She pulled the edge of the blinds aside enough to see who was out there on her back steps. Heddy. And next to her, a young man with hollow eyes burdened with grave disquiet. Soli ran to get the key from her coat pocket and unlocked the door.

Heddy put her arm around the young man's shoulders. "This is Jacob. He needs a safe place to sleep tonight. I thought he could stay in your special room in the basement."

CHAPTER EIGHT

SOLI OPENED THE DOOR wide and let them both in.

Heddy stepped in first, holding Jacob's hand. "He has nowhere to go. The boys will help him across the border to Sweden, but we cannot do it until tomorrow. Arvid and Birger are planning the route right now. We need fake papers for him and to notify people who'll receive him at the various posts along the way." She gave Soli a serious but concerned look. "Are you all right with this?"

Soli nodded. "Yes. Maybe you should stay the night, too?"

"No, I need to get back to the boys. The plan is to get him out of Oslo in the early morning hours, and we need to arrange for transport." She hugged Soli. "Thank you, my sweet friend."

Heddy snuck out the door as quickly as she'd appeared.

Soli turned to Jacob who was standing there, a handsome young man in his late teens, tall and thin as an aspen. His dark eyes were big but dull. Sadness surrounded his soul, and it seemed as if the slightest breeze would cause him to tremble like an aspen leaf in the wind.

"Like Heddy said, I have a most secret room. No one will find you there."

He said nothing, only nodded and followed her down the stairs into the basement. She pushed aside a bookcase to reveal a door to a room. She turned a key in the lock and invited Jacob inside.

His face softened as he took in all the paintings covering the walls. "My family has always loved art," he said.

"Then you and I will get along very well. I work with art, but it's also been my passion and joy in life. These paintings and the ones stacked up in the corner over there are all part of the shop upstairs. I alternate the showroom." She picked up some papers and books on the floor and piled them on a desk against the far wall. "You must be hungry. I'll be right back, Jacob."

Soli hurried upstairs and filled a plate with bread, a few slices of goat's milk cheese, and half a sausage. She pulled the blanket off her bed and grabbed a bottle of water before she headed back down the stairs.

Jacob sat on the chair by the desk, still admiring the art on the wall.

"There's a woolen blanket on the shelf over there. You can use it as a mattress, and here's another for cover. The floor may be a little cold this time of year." She placed the food and water on the desk. "I wish I'd known you were coming; I would've bought some more meat and vegetables. Please eat."

"This is much better than what I've had in a long

while." He grabbed the food with both hands and shoved it into his mouth.

"Slowly," Soli said. "You're probably so hungry it pains and causes a horrible nausea. But if you don't take it easy, you'll have problems keeping it down."

He nodded. "I've felt like I walk in a dark tunnel, not knowing where it leads, and the only thought in my head is if there's food on the other side. My stomach has growled louder than dogs outside the butcher's shop."

Soli pulled up a three-legged stool. "Tell me about yourself, Jacob."

He ran his fingers through his long, dark bangs and pushed them to the side. "I'm a Jew, and I feel as if everyone can see it, that it's written on my forehead." He pulled on the lapels of his worn-out jacket. "I've left my home, my family's gone, and these old clothes are all I have."

"I apologize for my ignorance, but how many Jews are here in our country?"

"A couple of years ago we were about two thousand. Now…" He shrugged. "I don't know now. Many are gone. The new government stamped our identification papers with a red letter J. Once we're registered, there's no way around it. They have our address, and our neighbors seem willing to tell on any Jew on the street. Friends and family have been taken away at gunpoint, forced to leave everything behind. We've been treated in degrading and inhumane ways."

Jacob was a good young man with his life ahead of him. She pushed back the tears, and folded her hands in her lap, pressing them together to distract herself from the pain in her heart that seemed to spread to her arms and legs.

"How did you manage?" she asked.

He gulped down the water and devoured half a slice of bread. "With the war, the propaganda against the Jews also started. Did you know that when Vidkun Quisling became prime minister two years ago, one of his first civil actions was to reinstate part of the constitution forbidding Jews in Norway?"

Ashamed of her own unawareness and inexperience, Soli listened intently, wanting to understand, searching her mind for reasoning behind the madness. But she found none. Her heart broke into a thousand pieces, thinking of what this young man must feel, knowing his relatives and friends had already been taken away. He had no information about where they were or if they would ever return. His only chance was to flee to a neighboring country, eastward to Sweden or across the sea to the west.

"No, I didn't know," she answered. "How can they ban people from their own country?"

"Well, they do, even if the Jews have lived here for generations. I was born here, as were my parents. Why such hatred and prejudice and hostility toward people of our faith?"

Soli could not hold back the tears any longer and let them run freely. "I'm afraid I don't understand why. Some stores and restaurants in Oslo are closed, and hateful words are painted on the windows. I've heard Jews have been deported and their properties confiscated. But where have they been taken?"

"We don't know. The frightful thing is none have returned." He pushed the empty plate away.

What would it be like not knowing where your family was or if they'd return? The weekend she spent with Far had given Soli the encouragement she needed to go on. What if she did not have that in her life?

"I've learned Hitler wants a pure race, but why I'll never understand, and I'll never agree with it." She shook her head and frowned. "What's a race, anyway? Aren't we all nations under the same sky and children of a God who cares?"

He folded his arms dejectedly. "How can God allow this war to happen and people to be wicked?"

She leaned forward and touched his arm. "God does not choose wickedness. Folks do. I have to believe that. If I didn't, this life wouldn't make sense to me."

Jacob buried his face in his hands and rocked back and forth. He looked up, his watery eyes wandering. "I'm sorry. It's just that I'm all alone. My entire family has either been taken away or fled the country. And I...I'm a hunted animal." He handed her his papers. "Look for yourself."

The red stamp with a J for Jew was the focal point. Soli paused as she read his name... *Jacob Isaac Ruber*.

"There's a Ruber family who used to live at Frogner. Are you related to them?" she asked.

He nodded, lips pursed. "My uncle Leon, my aunt, and three cousins were all taken away."

Soli drew a short breath. The young man sitting in front of her belonged to the family she was trying to help. Should she tell him about the ledger? Maybe he already knew. The way he spoke about their family, they might be close enough to share their secrets. She had to throw some hints to see if he had knowledge about the old journal.

"You said you and your relatives love art."

"Uncle Leon is an avid collector. As head of our family,

he had many antiques and heirlooms in his home." He paused for a moment, rubbing his chin. His face softened, as if memories of better times seeped in. "When I was young, the walls in the dining room were covered with beautiful art in aged frames. Being a young boy, I didn't have an interest in art. But I liked to sit and listen to the elders discussing the old masters. There was one I found especially interesting—a tale about a painting by the Dutch artist Peter Paul Rubens. The woman in the painting was supposedly our great-great-great...I don't remember how far back...but she was an ancestor of ours." He sent Soli a kind, contented smile. "One day, I could not contain my curiosity any longer. I had to see the painting of our foremother for myself. I snuck away, opened the door to the parlor, and found the painting hanging above a carved bureau. She was beautiful. At least, that's what I noticed. As I said, I was a kid, and an attractive woman was always interesting."

Soli gave him a teasing look. "You probably haven't changed your mind about that yet?"

He grinned. "No, I still like a pretty face." Then his smile vanished once again. He leaned back in the chair. "My knowledge of art is limited, but we all knew it was valuable and had belonged to the Ruber family since the early seventeenth century."

Soli sat up straight. It was as if a blindfold had been ripped from her eyes, and a hidden treasure had been revealed. Of course! The R did not stand for Isaac or Leon Ruber's surname but the baroque master painter Peter Paul Rubens. She should have guessed. The artist Rubens had lived in Antwerp during the baroque period, had used the chiaroscuro technique, and was one of the most influential painters in art history with over ten thousand works of art. Her thoughts spun like a runaway merry-go-round.

Jacob must have noticed her enthusiasm. He tipped his head to the side, his eyes bewildered but curious.

Soli leaned forward, clenching her hands on her knees. "Do you know what happened to this particular painting?"

"No, I haven't seen it for many years. The last time I visited my uncle, the oldest paintings had been replaced with other, simpler pieces. Maybe he sold them."

"But you don't believe that for a moment, do you?"

He stared at the floor. "No, they were part of our heritage, not something you sell." He looked up. "What do you think happens to art when people are deported?"

"The valuable pieces are usually confiscated by the Nazis."

Jacob rubbed his eyes and yawned. Ripping up thoughts about what had happened to his family was no doubt painful. She could help them by finding their missing treasures, but to do that, she had to dig a little deeper. Maybe Jacob remembered something that could help her further. She had to choose her words carefully, so as not to disclose information dangerous for him to know.

It broke her heart that she had to keep the truth from him. But at this stage of the game, she had to protect him from knowledge that could get him into trouble. His future was unstable enough, and she did not want to add possible interrogations about his family's most valuable possessions. She wanted to tell him the truth—that she believed some of his family's old art pieces were hidden, and she wanted to find them before the Germans did. Their enemies may have heard rumors and no doubt found bits of information. They seemed to have spies everywhere. She wanted to assure this young man that she was trying to stay a step ahead of Hitler, trying to find the artwork and take those valuables to a safe location.

But she didn't, and she dismissed the idea even though the thought of her tracing the treasured family painting would have sparked hope in Jacob.

He got up and paced the room. "My uncle has…or had, rather…an old book with our ancestral lineage written on the last page."

The ledger! Jacob had seen it. Soli hadn't had time to read all the way through yet, but the young man's information had clarified the Ruber family's lineage, the places they'd lived, and the art they'd collected. She could hardly wait to go back and get the old book out of Far's trunk, take it to her special spot in the woods, and continue studying it.

Jacob paused in his pacing. "Growing up, my cousins and I were taught about our religion, faith, and heritage. Uncle Leon showed us the ledger. Our genealogy goes back to an Italian Jew named Isaac Ruber, the one I and many others are named after. He was supposedly filthy rich and collected art from the most talented painters of his time."

If she could only tell him the ledger was safely hidden in a small house in the countryside, that she was the only one who knew where it was. But how could she? She'd better change the subject before she gave away the whereabouts of the old journal. If Jacob was ever questioned by anyone, he should not have to suffer because of his family's record book. For now, it was better not to say anything.

She lifted her chin and gave him a friendly smile. "Where've you been staying?"

"A friend put me up for a while, but with several razzias in the neighborhood, I didn't want him to get caught hiding me." Eyes filled with concern, he met Soli's gaze. "Are you sure you want to take the risk? People have had their houses burned down, been arrested and even shot for helping folks like me."

His life was in her hands. A while back, she would have been scared to death at the prospect of helping a fugitive, worried sick that someone would come barging through her back door, demanding she disclose where she was hiding him. But for some reason, words of assurance came out of her mouth without hesitation. "Yes, you'll be safe here."

And at that point in time, she meant it.

* * *

Soli pulled the duvet up under her chin and tossed back and forth. She could not find peace to fall into a quiet, contented sleep. What would it be like to be a young man like Jacob? Every citizen fifteen years and older had to carry identification papers and a passport. The system was effective for the Germans and gave them more control, but it made travel difficult and sometimes impossible for the average Norwegian. Soli always carried her cards, and it was hard enough having to show those papers at every checkpoint and on buses whenever demanded. The Jews were viewed as less than-human by the enemy, and they had a bright-red letter stamped on their papers. She couldn't fathom the thought of being treated that way... like cattle or stray dogs.

Sirens outside howled through the darkness. The sound came closer. Soli ran to the shop window in front and peeked out. A Gestapo car stopped a few meters from her door, and two men jumped out with flashlights in hand. She rapidly smoothed the blackout blind in place and leaned against the front door, her chest heaving. The beam from the flashlights glared through a small crack in the door. Marching boots stomped by the display window, and someone grabbed the door handle. The street fell silent. She held her breath. Did they know about Jacob? What would she say if they barged through her door? At least, she'd closed the hidden basement room and put the bookshelf back in place. There no way they'd find him.

A man yelled out in a brusque voice, *"Haben Sie den Schlingel gefunden?"*

Which rascal was he talking about? The young man in her basement? Just then, a shot sounded, and angry voices cut through the fog of night. A moment later, car doors slammed shut, and they drove off.

She crept away from the front door and crawled under the cover on her sofa-bed in the back room. Morning was merely a couple of hours away. She closed her eyes, pushed the fear away, and invited thoughts that made her heart happy. She'd figured out what the letter R stood for. The painter Peter Paul Rubens. She had to locate the treasured work of art and take it to safety before Hitler's spies found out about it. Oh, to see, to touch an original by a grand master like Rubens. In the middle of a tumultuous time, she could not help but smile with anticipation. But in the back of her mind, she knew the journey ahead would be filled with ravenous wolves from the Reich. Greedy animals who would stop at nothing to get the treasure for themselves.

~ CAPITOLO II ~
ANTWERP, 1613

FABIOLA FOUND HER padre in the parlor. He often sat there on early evenings, reading or taking a nap. Today, he was wide awake. He sat in one of the soft chairs with his arms folded in his lap. Puffy sleeves of brocade lay on his pleated overcoat, and his legs were stretched out.

"Hello, my sweet," he said and smiled. "You seem to be in good spirits."

He was growing older, and Fabiola worried whenever he had bouts of cough or leaned on a cane because his back ached.

She glanced over her shoulder, in the direction of his gaze, and smiled to herself. Apparently, her timing was perfect. Her padre sat and studied the painting of her on the wall.

"Padre, I know what I want for my birthday."

"Do you now? I'm not surprised." He patted the chair next to his. "Come, tell me. What would you like me to get you? Is this gift you desire within a reasonable frame?

I mean, you're not going to ask me for an elephant or a giraffe?"

Fabiola laughed. "No, it's absolutely something you can obtain and afford."

"Oh, that's good. Anything for you, *passerotta*."

She adored when he called her his little sparrow. It made her feel protected and loved.

"Padre, this is a gift for you as much as it is for me."

"Oh, well, I like the sound of that."

"You know how much you cherished having portraits done of my mother when she lived, and also paintings of me growing up?"

He nodded. "Those images are my favorite possessions."

"Well, I would like to have someone paint a portrait of Annarosa and me together."

His smile grew broader. "An excellent gift. We have not done one of you since we lived in Malta." He sat up straight and gave her a pensive expression. "But what about your husband? Should you not discuss this with him first?"

"You must have noticed what Eli is like. He has little interest in fine arts. Besides, he's away and won't be back before my birthday."

It was the truth. Eli spent his time maintaining and growing his wealth and good repute. The name Ruber opened doors for his business and strengthened his self-esteem. If she was to have exactly the portrait she desired, she needed the interest only her Padre could give.

He lifted his gaze to the painting on the wall and slowly nodded several times. Did he reminisce on good memories from when he went to the artist to commission the painting?

"Certainly, my lovely," he said and leaned back again. "I will see to it."

Her face lost all tension, and joy burst through her body. "Please, Padre, one more thing."

"Yes." He stretched the word. Padre had that air, that questioning, sideways glance when he expected her to ask for something he could not refuse. Because she was his only daughter, his *tesoro*, his treasure.

His behavior made her smile. How often had she used her feminine charm and the privilege of being his beloved offspring? They both knew it. But a grown woman now, she used that advantage with more caution.

"No, no, Padre. No more gifts. Only this one portrait. But please, may I choose the artist? You have no time for such trivial matters, and my good husband has no taste."

"Fabiola, you must never have him hear you utter such words. Criticizing your husband..." He frowned and waved his index finger at her.

"But, Padre, it's true. Have you not seen the brown vase he purchased for my last anniversary, or the painting he traded as an investment, that horrible boat scene by an unknown and untalented painter?"

Padre put his hands on his belly and laughed loud. "I see what you mean." His lips pursed in a fine line. "You don't know many people in Antwerp. How will you find the right one?"

"I'll find a way." She took both his hands in hers. "Please..."

"I've not seen you this enlivened in a long time. It pleases me." He raised his chin and said in a determined voice, "So be it. You may choose your artist."

She threw her arms around his neck. "Oh, thank you,

Padre. He'll be a most brilliant one, and you will be both delighted and proud. Wait and see."

She leaped to her feet, swished out of the room, and made her way through the corridors toward the nursery, but it was empty. She hurried down the stairs and into the garden. There was her little angel with Hester, the nurse-maid. Fabiola picked up Annarosa and twirled her around.

"You and I will go on an adventure together. Would you like that?"

The child squealed as they whirled around the grounds. Fabiola loved this little being with all her heart. Spending time with Annarosa was pure joy and gave Fabiola hope for their future in a new land and with a husband she still did not really know.

TUESDAY, 3 OCTOBER 1944

CHAPTER NINE
OSLO, NORWAY

BEFORE SUNRISE THE next morning, Soli wandered sleepily around her back room, picking up clothing she'd stepped out of the night before. Rain pattered steadily on the windowpane, but then she heard footsteps outside the door. She stopped and listened. A double knock two times calmed her. She glanced out into obscurity. No light struggled to get through the heavy clouds, but she recognized the shapes of Heddy's boys. They'd come for Jacob.

She rubbed her eyes, pulled on her blue robe, and unlocked the door.

Birger stood in front, a big grin on his freckled face as usual.

"My goodness, Birger! They let you out." Soli hugged him fiercely. "When you were arrested at the raid in the crypt, I was afraid—"

Arvid stood tall and stout behind his friend. "They let him out a couple of days ago. Seems they didn't consider him as a threat."

Birger grabbed his suspenders and straightened his back. "Little do they know, I'm right back in the game," he said and chuckled.

She pretended not to notice a tooth missing in his charming smile. His oversized shoes and clothes looked bigger than before, and she could tell underneath the outer cheerfulness that the weeks he'd spent in detention at Grini had been rough on him.

"I'm so happy to see you, Birger, come on in."

"Hey, how about me?" Arvid followed Birger inside, his broad shoulders almost too wide for her narrow back door.

Soli smiled. She always felt safe with him around.

"Of course, I'm thrilled to see you, too, Arvid." She closed the door behind them. "You're here for our new friend?"

"Yes. Heddy always says there's safety in moving during the night. She sends women out during the day and men at night."

"Well, Heddy knows what she's doing. You have the escape route planned?"

"Yes, we'll hurry up the back roads to the park behind the royal palace. There'll be a car waiting for us there." Birger shifted his feet. "We need to get going as quickly as possible."

"And you have new papers for Jacob?"

Arvid patted his pocket. "All in order, thanks to our good friend, Nikolai, at the police station."

How Nikolai managed all the extra work for the resistance in addition to his work as an inspector was incredible. Every time Soli heard his name, emotional warmth spread through her body.

"Soli?" Arvid was staring at her.

"Yes. I'll get Jacob," she said and hurried down the stairs to the secret room in the basement.

She found Jacob wide awake sitting on the mattress on the floor.

"I heard voices," he said and stood. "I'm ready to go."

As they reached the top of the stairs, Soli grabbed his shoulder. "I noticed your jacket. It's worn, and colder weather is on the way."

"I know, but it's all I own."

She rushed into the office, grabbed a navy-blue peacoat jacket off a hook behind the door, and handed it to Jacob.

"Here, try this on. It belonged to the man who had the art shop before. It's in good shape, and the coarse wool should keep you warm."

The coat fit him to perfection. Jacob gave Soli a grateful nod and followed her to the back room.

"Do you have anything else you need to bring?" Arvid asked.

Jacob shook his head. "No, I didn't have time."

"Good. It will be easier without luggage. A suitcase would only be in the way. When you get across the Swedish border, there'll be other people to provide you with food and clothing."

Soli emptied her shoulder bag on the floor, brought it to the small kitchen cabinet in the corner of the room, and stuffed three bottles and a couple of paper bags into her sack. "I made this late last night. You'll be hungry, and this should be enough for the three of you for a day or two."

Birger stepped forward. "But, Soli, we couldn't."

She handed him the shoulder bag. "No 'buts'. I can share. Today, you boys need it more than I do."

Arvid touched Birger's shoulder. "You know better than to contradict her. She usually knows best."

She winked at Arvid then hugged them all again. "Now, hurry."

Birger nudged Jacob. "Come on. We must go."

As they stepped out the door, Jacob turned one last time. His hollow eyes stared at Soli, but the corners of his mouth pulled into a tired grin. "God bless you."

She smiled back at him. "And you, Jacob. Stay safe."

***

Soli probably should have gone back to sleep for an hour, but instead, she chose to finish some frames for a regular, the wife of a German officer who browsed the store most weeks. Soon, she would open the shop and greet customers with a professional and, hopefully, wakeful presence.

By three o'clock, the jingle above the door became less frequent. Soli welcomed the chance to sink into a comfortable chair in the front room. She kicked off her shoes and propped up her feet next to a stack of art history books on the low table. She'd barely closed her eyes when the bell jingled again.

"And here I thought you were busy working." Nikolai stood in front of her. He winked and threw her off guard with his smile.

She plopped her feet onto the floor and stood. "Well, I—"

"Sit back own, Soli. I happen to know what you did all night." He pulled up the other soft chair and sat. "But we need to touch base on what's going on with the ledger. What have you found out?"

Soli resumed her seat. "I'm not telling you where the old book is."

He put his hands up. "Good. It's safe, and that's all I need to hear." He leaned forward. "You mentioned at the auction you'd detected another missing painting."

The prospect of finding an art treasure, especially one from the seventeenth century, made her heart leap. She told Nikolai about her discoveries in Henry Gran's notebooks, the curious numbers in the margin of the ledger, and her conversation with Jacob.

"What about Lieutenant Colonel Heinz Walter? Did you find out why he's here?" she asked.

"From what I've heard, he's still in the country. I don't trust him for a second. What he's doing with Sophus Bech is another question. Walter is an art fanatic, obsessed with new finds, and he'll stop at nothing to get his way. He may be using the young protégé to spy for him."

Soli shivered. "I don't like that thought." She straightened up. "Would you like a cup of tea, Nikolai?"

"No, thank you. But before I go...I had a talk with Heddy yesterday. She's having dinner with a prominent Nazi today."

Soli's mind was suddenly tossed into a swirl. Heddy tried to avoid the national socialists, both Norwegian and German, at all costs, and her obscure life consisted of never-ending plans to thwart the enemy from progressing. She certainly clocked more hours than any of them when it came to obstructing the Nazis.

Dread seemed to seize Soli's body, and a tight lump of pain formed in the pit of her stomach. An alarmed voice in her head told her to find Heddy and tell her not to do it. *Don't walk into the lion's den.* The thought of Heddy spending time with a high-level Nazi was intolerable.

Soli grabbed Nikolai's arm. "Why would Heddy do that? She must have a good reason. Who is he?"

Nikolai took hold of her hand, his eyes locked on hers, and with a gentle voice he said, "Her father, Carl Vengen."

CHAPTER TEN

HEDDY LEFT HER cousin's apartment and took the streetcar to meet her father. She'd run into him by the town hall the day before, and he'd suggested lunch at a restaurant called Amundsen's.

The platform was crowded, and she stood away from other people. The ride into Oslo took about fifteen minutes. She was the last one to get on and the last off, which gave her a better view of other passengers so she could make sure no one followed her.

Heddy rounded the corner of Roald Amundsen Street, named after the Norwegian explorer who'd led the first expedition to the South Pole thirty-some years earlier. She stopped to check her reflection in the window of a laundry shop. Her father would probably not approve of her black pants and flat shoes, so she'd added a scarf with red flowers to give her appearance a more feminine touch. She removed the beret, smoothed her hair into place, and added another layer of bright-red lipstick to her mouth. It would have to do. Regardless of how much her father wanted it, she could not be someone other than herself.

Amundsen's had a reputation for dishing up good meals but also served mostly those who sympathized with Hitler and his vision. One of the primary reasons it attracted the Nazi elite was the constant flow of alcohol. Heddy let out a long, exasperated sigh. *Profiteers.* She could vomit just thinking about them—the people who earned large amounts of money by making themselves available to the occupying forces. Men who had access to machines, property, and even liquor. The owner of Amundsen's was such a man. As chairman of the board of the government-owned Wine Monopoly, he took advantage of being in the pocket of the Germans. He'd made his fortune at the expense of others, and he did not seem to worry about the outcome of the war or the welfare of his fellow countrymen.

A few years ago, the establishment had been a quaint cafeteria owned by two Jewish brothers. Now, they were gone, probably arrested, and the place had been turned into a Nazi-friendly establishment. That, too, was a fact that made Heddy's stomach churn. The meal, no matter how delicious, was already doomed to taste like sawdust.

Heddy relaxed her fists and pushed the door open. She could not put off this meeting any longer. The spacious restaurant had dark furniture and starched white linen tablecloths. Chandeliers hung from the ceiling, adding sophisticated class to the room. Where was her father? She stretched her neck, trying to locate where he sat. Oh, my goodness. There he was, at a table in the far corner. At least, they would not be in the center for everyone to observe, but how would she get out if a problem arose? She scanned the room for other exits. Through the kitchen was an option. Also, next to the bar was a side door to the street.

Her father stood as she approached and even pulled a chair out for her to sit. Not much taller than herself, he looked distinguished as always with his pin-striped suit and round, dark-rimmed glasses. His hair was grayer than she remembered, and his belly a little rounder. Whatever the circumstances, he'd had enough to eat.

He gathered a small pile of documents in front of him, turned them upside down, and placed them on the edge of the table by the wall. Snapping his fingers at a waitress, he sat.

The waitress came and curtsied.

"We'll have a bottle of your good dry." His voice was deep and demanding.

"Yes, sir." The waitress trudged across the floor to the bar, no doubt tired of remarks about her narrow waist and the constant pats on her behind delivered by red-faced customers.

The young woman returned with the bottle and handed him a menu, but he shoved the *carte du jour* aside.

"We'll have the pork chops with stewed peas, potatoes, and lingonberries."

No surprise, he ordered without asking her what she preferred. He'd always been the resolute leader both at home and at work; one could say unflinching. She answered by fixing him with an unwavering stare.

At first, he ignored her but then said, "You're nothing like your mother and sisters, Hedvig."

He didn't mean the statement as a compliment. Heddy's mother had been patient and gentle, and the two younger sisters had never raised their voices at him.

She poured herself a glass of water and took a sip. "More like you, then, Father?"

He raised his hands in denial. "Oh, no. You're your own person. I'm not to blame for how you turned out."

To avoid criticism and, more importantly, any questions about what she was doing nowadays, Heddy asked him about his life and profession. Answering her kept him busy. He seemed proud of his merits and the progress within the ministry of communications between the Reich's departments in Oslo and Berlin. She did her utmost to enjoy her meal, which was the best she'd had in a long time. Listening mostly, she said little but behaved politely to dodge any more confrontations.

The atmosphere in the restaurant was less desirable. She scanned the room while her father spoke. An enemy sat on every seat. People who worked for a dictator she despised. Her life the last few years had been spent working against the Führer's system. Countless times she'd put not only her own life but the lives of her friends in danger.

Heddy startled as two men in Gestapo uniforms rushed in the main door. One blew a whistle, and the other went from one table to another. The second man sounded agitated. What was he saying?

"One moment, dear," her father said. "Stay here. I'll find out what's going on."

Dear? He'd called her dear. He had not done that since she was a young girl. What made him protective all of a sudden? Was he trying to set her up and make her open up and reveal things about her life? Heddy was not that gullible. She looked around the room. What were her options? There was no place to hide. One of the men still stood by the front door. The other interrogated the couple at the table next to the bar.

Her father strode across the floor and gesticulated as he spoke with the soldier by the second exit. Should she make a run toward the outhouse in the back yard? Heddy bit her lip then turned over the documents on the table. She gazed toward the exit. Her father was still occupied, waving his arms and talking. She flipped through the papers. There were photographs of artwork, Jewish surnames, names of galleries and museums. *The Ministry of Communications, my foot.* What was her father doing with information about art in Norway? At the bottom of the page, someone had scribbled Lieutenant Colonel Heinz Walter's name and a phone number.

She rapidly put the pages back in place and peeked across the room. Father turned back in her direction, smiling and nodding to people at adjacent tables as if to assure them everything was fine. The two German soldiers marched into the kitchen. There was a skirmish in the back, sounds of pots and pans falling onto the floor, people shouting, and glass breaking. Before long, the soldiers returned, pushing a handcuffed man in front of them. A tearful older woman tried to follow. One of the military men forced her back into the kitchen, and the door was slammed shut in her face. The soldiers then pulled the handcuffed fellow out the front door and left.

And with that, and the guests in the restaurant returned to their meals and resumed their friendly conversations.

"Sorry about that, Hedvig. A standard razzia. That's all it was."

She barely dared ask but had to know. "Who were they after?"

"Oh, just a regular roundup, I suppose. Some people who have been bombed out of their homes work in kitchens and at other odd jobs around the city. Not all of them are friendly to the reformed constitution." He leaned back in the chair and snapped his fingers again, obviously ready for dessert this time.

To Heddy, he continued to speak in an eloquent manner, although she would have used words like "invasion" and phrases such as "robbing people of their freedom." Of course, a person would react to having home and livelihood stripped away. Free will and autonomy were worth fighting for. Integrity was not a weakness. It was what breathed life into her dreary, war-infected days.

"Your dessert, sir." The waitress placed two small bowls with rhubarb porridge and cream in front of them.

Soli had not finished her dinner yet and asked the waitress to leave her plate a while longer. Her father continued his monologue about life as an outstanding representative of the Reich. As he was in the middle of a story about deporting prisoners, a man approached their table. He clicked his heels together and bent over to whisper something to her father.

"Aha, yes...yes." Her father nodded while making affirmative grunts.

The man, in his early thirties, was clean-shaven and seemed proper. He removed his hat, revealing short-cropped, stiff hair with a receding line at the temples. But what did first impressions mean? Heddy could only follow her intuition, and her perception of the man warned her of trouble. He stole glances toward Heddy, while talking into her father's ear. Deep-set gray eyes intently stared at her. Did he know who she was and what she did?

She had a clear path to the exit door by the bar now.

Sitting on the edge of her seat, she poured herself some more water from the jug.

Finally, the young man straightened up, smoothed the tablecloth, his eyes still fixed on Heddy. He bowed, clicked his heels once again, and left the restaurant, slightly dragging his right leg.

Heddy leaned forward. "Who was that?"

Her father shoved the last spoonful of dessert into his mouth. "My assistant, Sophus Bech, a bright but irritatingly pedantic fellow."

"He stared at me. It was uncomfortable."

Her father gave her a wry smile. "I'd like to see him call upon you, so you two may become better acquainted."

She clasped her hands in her lap and swallowed hard. "He's not my type, Father."

"Why not? The man has a promising future. He's extremely successful in his career. One could say he's up and coming. What's not to like? Being a woman, you must have noticed his good looks."

Heddy was drowning and could hardly wait to get out of the smoke-filled restaurant teeming with guests she usually did her best to avoid. She had to round up this conversation and get out of there. "Yes, he's handsome, but I am still not interested."

Her father was not about to give up yet. "I'll arrange a meeting. It'll be good for you. You look way too serious. Have some fun, girl."

She placed two flat palms on the table and looked him in the eye. "No, Father. I'm a grown woman and capable of choosing my own dates. My goodness, we don't live in the Medieval Ages."

He frowned. "How is it possible you've become even more outspoken than you were growing up?"

She leaned back in her seat and kept a soft tone in her voice. "I apologize, Father. I found it distressing the way he stared. Promise me you won't speak about me to your assistant."

He shrugged. "Very well. But don't take his behavior the wrong way. Sophus stares at all beautiful women, and you are attractive, Hedvig. Surely, you can understand that men would be interested. For all I know, you may already have someone special in your life." He straightened his back and gave her a crooked smile. "If so, I'd like to meet him, see if he's good enough for my daughter and all that."

She chose not to reply. The man she loved worked against everything her father stood for. Even though she missed Sverre every hour of the day, she was glad he was in Stockholm, far away from the German-occupied environment she had to live in. The risk of having him return now was too great. Besides, what did her father know about having one special person in his life? Heddy had understood from a young age that her father kept company with other women. She'd never heard her parents quarrel. Not once had her mother mentioned the fact that he was unfaithful, but Heddy had known.

Her father broke her train of thought. "I did not want to speak in front of my assistant. You have always been strong-willed, more than I would have wanted in a daughter. If you could only use that persistence and stamina to—"

"Oh, Father. Please."

How many times had she heard those words growing up? He had three daughters. The oldest one should have been a son who carried on the name.

He threw his hands up. "All right. I don't know what

you are up to, Hedvig, but in my book, it's no good. You have a rebellious disposition. I cannot protect you from yourself. I'd never attempt to harm you. No matter what you think about my efforts to be a decent father, I care for you." His eyes narrowed. "But if you go against our new leaders, I'll do my duty and stop you."

Heddy wrapped the potato she had left on her dinner plate in a napkin and slipped it into her pocket. "Goodbye, Father. I wish you well. I really do." She got to her feet. Head held high, she walked out of the restaurant and never looked back.

CHAPTER ELEVEN

SOLI RECEIVED A note from a messenger in the late afternoon to meet Heddy at the Cemetery of Our Savior a few minutes' walk from the royal palace. She locked up the shop after work and hurried toward the National Theatre and the *Storting*, the German-occupied parliament building. The huge red banner with the black swastika made her shiver every time she passed by. She deliberately kept her eyes straight forward and turned left onto Oslo's parade street, Karl Johan's. By the time she passed through the iron gate at the cemetery, she was ready to remove her scarf and open the buttons on her blue coat. She pulled off her hat and shook her head. The fresh air gave new energy after a day inside the shop with demanding customers and new orders for both art and handmade frames. She didn't complain. A busy day of work produced a good living.

The rain had let up a couple of hours earlier, but even though the grass was drying up, she stayed on the graveled paths. She wore her sturdy dark-brown shoes and black socks. The fish-skin shoes tended to fall apart if they got wet. Soli passed by the gravestones of important men in Norwegian culture; the playwright Henrik Ibsen, who'd reaped great fame far outside the Norwegian borders in his own time; Bjornstjerne Bjornson, a writer whose lyrics to *Ja, vi elsker dette landet*, their national anthem, had more meaning now than ever before. The man had even received the Nobel Prize in Literature for his poetry. And Edward Munch, gifted and significant painter who'd passed away only eight months earlier. All three great men with great influence.

Heddy sat on a bench, staring into space. Dark circles discolored the skin beneath her eyes. Her fatigue came from far more than lack of sleep. Soli plopped down and hooked her arm around Heddy's.

"How are you? Nikolai told me you had an appointment with your father earlier today."

Heddy swallowed hard but sat in silence. Soli pulled Heddy's arm even closer.

After a minute or two, Heddy spoke. "I know there are many uncomfortable tasks for us, times when I've felt like we're in a small rowboat in the middle of the sea, and dark storm clouds are rolling in. Then a tempestuous wind takes hold of that small vessel, ready to toss us overboard to be swallowed up by the raging, unforgiving waves." A shiver shot through Heddy's body. "But going into that restaurant today…people who glorify the Reich at every table, and the owner of the restaurant, who didn't do all that well before the war broke out, but who now makes a generous living from his collaboration with the enemy…it makes me sick to my stomach."

"Then why did you do it?"

"He's my father. My family. I thought maybe it would improve my relationship with him to see him."

"Couldn't you have met somewhere else?"

Heddy shook her head. "Not without throwing suspicion that I avoid places like that. Besides, he chose where to eat, and my opinion would've had no impact."

Soli glanced around to see if anyone else could listen in. Two older ladies were tending the flowers by a gravestone farther down the path. It was safe to speak.

"So, what did you learn today?" Soli asked.

Heddy told her about the razzia at the restaurant, the sudden appearance of her father's assistant, and the papers on the table.

Soli frowned. "Those papers... You say they were all art related?"

"They were. Auctions from Jewish households with lists of paintings, china, and such. Names of galleries, names of famous Norwegian painters and sculptors. Why the sudden interest in art? My father has mostly worked in administrative positions and dealt with communication and diplomacy. And Heinz Walter's name written at the bottom." She gave Soli a disgusted face. "I hoped we'd seen the last of the lieutenant colonel."

Soli slowly shook her head. "I'm afraid not. I saw him at the auction last night."

Heddy gawked. "What? Did he speak to you?"

"No, fortunately not. I don't think he even saw me. I noticed him as he walked out the door. I double-checked with Nikolai, hoping I was wrong. But it was certainly him."

Heddy straightened up. "Well, we'll have to prepare for

another storm. We've survived Heinz Walter before; we'll do so again if we must."

Soli patted Heddy's arm. "We will. But tell me more about your father's assistant. You said he stared at you."

"He did. When I think about it, I believe he's the same man who followed me last Friday morning."

"But you said you didn't see his face then."

"No, but he had the same straight posture and walked with that limping gate, as if one leg was stiff or hurt. I wonder what he's up to."

Shock coursed through Soli's body.

Heddy must have noticed Soli's change of expression. "What is it, Soli?

"I've met him."

Heddy narrowed her eyes. "You have? Where?"

"At the auction yesterday. That man has the most penetrating stare. His name is Sophus Bech, isn't it?"

"Correct."

Soli leaned forward, elbows on knees, and rested her head in her hands. "You know what this means? These men, your father, his assistant Sophus Bech, Henry Gran, and now, Lieutenant Colonel Heinz Walter...most likely, they're all looking for the Ruber family's missing painting. Are they collaborating?"

"If they are, I've no doubt you'll find out."

Soli leaned back on the bench and gently punched Heddy's shoulder. "*We'll* find out."

"Well, I'll have the boys keep a look-out for Sophus Bech. I've a bad feeling about him." Heddy pulled a napkin-wrapped parcel out her pocket. She placed it on her lap, revealing a potato. "This is for you, Soli. I wish I could've shared the whole plate with you."

Soli picked up the vegetable and took a bite. Juice from the pork chop had soaked into the potato, a heavenly taste she'd not had for a while. She hesitated before eating more, but Heddy nudged Soli's shoulder.

"Go ahead, eat. I'm still full."

The food was cold, but Soli relished the flavor. Still concerned about Carl Vengen, she asked, "Heddy, your father actually said he'd stop you?"

"He did, but it was obvious he doesn't know how deeply I'm engaged in the resistance effort. That's one reason it's so important to use a codename. Not even so-called loved ones should know about our involvement. For one thing, knowing what we do could draw them into danger." Heddy twisted her fingers in her lap.

Soli placed her hand on Heddy's to calm her. "The other thing is that a loved one could expose what we do and jeopardize or even imperil *our* lives."

"Exactly. It's a horrible thought, but that's what it is. I've my father to worry about; you've got your aunt and uncle."

"I know, but Uncle Charles works in an office. He became a Nazi because my aunt thought it was the safe thing to do. Not to mention, Uncle Charles doesn't hold a high position like your father does."

"Even the littlest sliver can cause great pain and even infection, Soli."

Heddy was right. They could never let their guards down but push forward with caution, always looking over their shoulders.

Across from them, two squirrels disappeared into a hollow in the tree. Soli stared at the dark cave and thought of something Heddy had spoken of earlier.

"When he said you have a rebellious disposition, what did he mean?"

With a touch of scorn, Heddy said, "I never became an architect, a doctor, or a lawyer. That was important to him." She turned to Soli with a soft gaze. "You managed to finish your degree, even with a war going on."

"I had to take several backroads to finish it. But remember, that's all I did during those years. I never gave the war resistance a single thought. Art history filled my whole life. You, on the other hand, were involved in fighting our enemy from the day they placed foot on our land. One day, Heddy...one day, this war will be over, and you can pursue any education you choose."

"Sweet Soli, you are incurably optimistic." Heddy stood.

"Do you have time to go by the chiffer group tonight?"

Heddy straightened her beret. "I do. In fact, we can go right now if you like."

Soli jumped up. The prospect of finding more clues ignited a spark of optimism. "I can tell you what I've discovered so far on the way there. Henry Gran had some theories in the making, and there may be more to find in the papers in their office."

They started toward the iron gate at the edge of the cemetery. Out on the street ahead, a group of soldiers jumped onto the back of a truck and drove off. Two young mothers pushed their prams in the other direction. Did they have illegal newspapers hidden under their babies? Were they on a covert mission right under the noses of the Germans who'd just driven off? Maybe not, but the thought that she was not alone fighting the occupying forces was comforting. Anyone out there could be on her side.

She'd never thought much about where Heddy slept at night. Now, with all the talk about Heddy's father, Soli could not help but wonder.

"Heddy, I don't know where you live, but what about you father? I mean, are you safe in case he finds out about your work?" A series of anxious *what-ifs* raced through her mind. She turned to Heddy and almost in a whisper said, "Does your father know where you live?"

Heddy kept walking, seemingly not as worried as Soli —at least, not on the surface. "No, I hardly know where I live anymore. Heaven knows, I change locations often enough."

Soli pushed that worry aside. There was enough trouble to be concerned with. As they exited the cemetery, she leaned in and said low, "With Sophus Bech working for your father, and your father collaborating with Heinz Walter we're in for double trouble."

"I'm afraid so."

"What do we do now?"

"We need to make sure my father never discovers what his daughter is involved with."

* * *

Z opened the door and let them in. "Hello, girls. I'm all alone here tonight."

Heddy closed the door behind them. "You still haven't heard from Henry Gran?"

Z shook her head. "Not a word. But communication can be difficult these days. I hope he's all right, but I must say I worry about him."

"As do we." Heddy pulled up a couple of chairs by the

large table covered in papers. "Elsie has some questions for you. We were hoping you could help us out."

"Certainly. I'll try."

They all sat, and Soli wrote the fourteen numbers from the ledger on a scrap of paper.

"I can't tell you where I found this number, but we need help figuring out what they mean. Could you take a look at them?"

Z lowered her brows. "A foreign phone number or a code or number for an item?" She picked up the note. "May I keep this for a couple of days and report back to you?"

"Yes, of course. I'm happy to have your help." Soli pulled out the scrunched-up paper they'd found in Henry Gran's apartment from her pocket. "I've one more thing." She flattened the paper on the table. "I believe this is to read a code. The little squares are cut out by hand. Do you have something here you'd use it for?"

Z slowly shook her head. "No, it's an easy way to make a code, but we haven't had anything like this for a long time. Since we got the machine, we do most of our cryptography that way."

Soli twisted her hands in her lap.

Z leaned forward. "I can tell you're thinking hard. Keep letting those thoughts roll around in your head, then grab the foremost idea and start there."

Soli grabbed a clean piece of lined paper and started writing down letters. They were in no order and made no sense, but she wrote what she saw in her mind. She was careful with letter-spacing and font size as if she wrote the text on a checkered piece of paper. Once she'd written ten complete lines, she grabbed the crumbled paper and placed it on top. She traced her fingers along the openings and read the letters. "T,w,o,b,r,o,t,h,e,r,s."

"Two brothers? What does that mean?" Heddy asked.

"No idea yet. But I've a strong feeling it's important to what we're working on."

"I don't need to know where you found those letters," Z said. "It's better we don't carry everyone's secret projects. And I've not come across *two brothers* before. Try placing the crumbled paper upside down."

Soli did as she was asked, but the letters that showed up made no sense.

Z picked up the crumbled code paper. "Could there be another way to use it?" She turned the code paper backward and covered Soli's writing again.

"B...a...r...o...q...u...e...a...r...t...s." Z read each letter out loud.

"Baroque arts," Soli said. "That makes sense."

"Yes, it does. Thanks, Z. We appreciate your time." Heddy touched her shoulder. "Soli, we should go. It's getting late."

"Of course." Soli stood and put her coat and hat on. She gave Z a hug. "Thank you, Z. Every bit helps."

Walking down the path to the road, Heddy said, "Your memory is amazing. I'd get lost before I'd finished the first line of random letters. Where did you pick up that information?"

"Henry Gran's notebooks. There was one page that looked different from all the others. I took Z's advice and worked with my intuition. This time, I was in luck. Now, if I can only figure out what the words mean."

* * *

Soli and Heddy split up on the corner near the old department store. Soli had no idea where Heddy went to spend the night but prayed for her friend's safety.

She passed the old church with the crypt and crossed Karl Johan's Street. As she approached the next corner, she felt a sudden blow from behind. Someone shoved her forcefully into a nearby brick wall, grabbed her purse, and ran away.

She struggled back onto her feet. Brushing the dirt off her clothes, she realized how sore her upper left arm was, and her knee throbbed from hitting the sidewalk. Blood seeped out where her new nylon stockings were torn. It was a superficial but painful wound. Shocked and confused, Soli looked up and down the street. Who had rammed her?

The perpetrator was long gone. Tempting as it was, she did not call for help. She could not have someone ask questions about where she'd been. The assault had happened too fast to have caused her much fear, but that soon changed as Soli limped home alone through the damp fog. Where was Nikolai when she needed him? Looking over her shoulder, she feared she was being followed and rushed down the lane to the back of the shop. Not until she was safely inside and had pushed the table in front of the locked door, did she relax her shoulders.

Luckily, she always carried the keys to the art shop in her pocket and her identification papers tucked in a pocket inside her coat. What about the contents of her purse? There was not much she'd miss—a pair of knitted mittens, scissors, a handkerchief, a lipstick, and a pen. Good thing she'd given Jacob her larger shoulder bag. She'd always carried more stuff around when she had it.

The purse had been a gift from her aunt Sigrid but not Soli's favorite.

Who had pushed her down? Did the thief think she had money? She rubbed her injured left arm, sniffed, and wrinkled her nose. Was that the smell of Old Spice? She lifted her arm to her face and sniffed again. The odor was there, faint but unmistakable.

~ CAPITOLO III ~
ANTWERP, 1613

FABIOLA'S PADRE had been coughing for a week.

A physician came to the house. "An illness of the chest," the old, bearded man concluded.

One did not have to be a trained doctor to make that diagnosis. Padre made wheezing sounds when he breathed, and he spent more time napping in the good chair in the parlor.

Fabiola tried poultice-making. She asked the cook to help her in the kitchen. Raw onions sliced and placed in a piece of linen should calm the cough. She added drops of lavender extract to make the scent more pleasant, and the purple floral stems helped reduce his anxiety and helped him rest.

She accompanied Padre's reliable assistant Gillis van Hoye to the chemist for herbal concoctions. The man knew the town implicitly, and he had personal acquaintances in every corner of Antwerp. Padre had complete faith in Gillis's sound judgement. Fabiola saw beyond the kind but firm brown eyes, the long nose, and his dark hair, graying at the temples. Gillis was trustworthy. He wore a black padded doublet with a soft white ruff around his neck, and Fabiola had the impression he was respected by all.

The apothecary suggested dried eucalyptus leaves for tea and a combination of thyme and oregano to blend with foods. Fabiola brought the herbs home and prepared the remedies. She boiled water and added peppermint leaves, covered his head with a cloth, and allowed the steam to float into his nostrils. It helped ease the tightness in his chest. She opened Padre's window often, as the cool air seemed to relieve the symptoms.

And every day, she kneeled with Annarosa, praying for *Nonno* to get better.

One morning, Padre, Fabiola, and Annarosa sat in the dining room when Gillis entered with a small bottle of sage and honey elixir for the throat.

He placed it on the table and turned to Fabiola. "I've done the research as you requested of me and went by the Guild of St. Luke today."

Fabiola leaned forward, curious what news Gillis had for her. "I understand the guilds are organized for the artisans and merchants to protect their trade and work, but who belongs to the Guild of St. Luke?"

Although she loved studying new things, she led such a sheltered life and was not aware of the events in town. Whenever the opportunity arose to ask and learn, she embraced it.

"Painters and artists are part of that league," Gillis said. "It's been around for two hundred and thirty years, and the guild keeps a list of students, artists, and those honored with the title of master."

"Did you find a suitable artist for my painting?"

Fabiola handed him a plate with slices of freshly baked bread.

Gillis grabbed a slice and took a bite. "I'm reliably informed and have visited painters here in Antwerp. Adam van Noort is one of them. He used to serve as dean of the Guild of St. Luke."

"What does he paint?" Padre asked.

"He's known for his religious paintings."

Fabiola frowned. "But I don't want a painting of me with a halo over my head or Annarosa as a cherub with wings. Can you find an artist who paints portraits of us mortal people?"

"Of course." Gillis rubbed his beard. "Hmm. Let me see. Adam van Noort has an apprentice called Jacob Jordeans, also born and bred here. The lad's barely twenty summers and has already been predicted a shining future."

"Has he studied under any Italian artists?"

"No, I don't believe he has, but he's gifted."

"That's well, but I'm looking for a certain style of painting."

"Very well, Signora. I'll find out more and report tomorrow, yes?"

"Tomorrow is fine."

Fabiola did not worry if it took a week or a month to locate the right painter. She had the image already in her mind and needed an artist who could paint that exact scene with the necessary technique.

The nursemaid came for Annarosa as Gillis left. Fabiola helped Padre up from the table, held his arm, and guided him into the parlor. She read poetry and sonnets to him by the Jewish-Italian authoress Devorà Ascarelli. And when he fell asleep, she sat with him, praying he would wake up with better health.

* * *

The next morning, Fabiola sat with her padre in the parlor when Gillis came by with more suggestions.

"I visited a few more studios yesterday and this morning. Frans Francken is known for his mythological renditions. He does excellent work." He kissed the joined tips of his fingers and spread them outward.

He must have noticed Fabiola's apprehension and continued.

"Joos de Momper paints astounding landscapes. He is a third-generation landscape artist and is already a master of the Guild of St. Luke." Gillis snickered. "You should have seen his studio, Signora. The man has fathered ten children, and they—"

Fabiola shook her head. "Please, I do not need a landscape painter or one who paints allegorical or religious themes."

Padre started coughing and pulled the sleeve on her burgundy gown. "May I speak with you, Daughter?"

"Of course." She turned to Gillis. "Will you please excuse us for a moment?"

Gillis bowed and left the room.

Padre leaned forward. "What ails you, Fabiola? The artists he speaks of are all talented and gifted. You seem uneasy, as if nothing is right."

"Oh, Padre. I know exactly what I want. My stomach seeks to purge itself with talk of landscapes, grotesque mythological beings, and idyllic ice-skating scenes on the river Schelde."

"I see. Then show him the painting in the parlor, *passerotta*," Padre said lovingly. "You seem to cherish that more than any other artwork in our house. Explain in plain words so he knows what you are talking about."

She bent down and kissed him and ran then into the hallway.

"Gillis, will you please accompany me into the parlor?"

The man followed her across the black-and-white marble floor and into the parlor, where she stopped in front of her portrait from Malta.

"I'd like someone who paints like this," she said.

"But, Signora, that is painted by the great Caravaggio."

She nodded. "It is."

"Caravaggio is dead, Signora. He passed away in Italy three summers ago."

"I'm aware of that. But many have followed in his footsteps, artists who saw the brilliance in his artistic performance, who admired him, and learned from his expertise. The painting must be done by someone who understands chiaroscuro and is gifted enough to use this technique."

Gillis raised his eyebrows and smiled. "Ah, I know who to ask, and he lives right here in Antwerp."

Fabiola sighed with relief. Was it possible? An artist of the caliber and level of ability she was searching for? And she would not have to travel far to go see him.

"Hopefully, you're correct," she said. "If the portrait does not resemble the work of Caravaggio, I'd rather not have one done at all."

"In his early years, this artist made a couple of trips to Rome and studied the art of Titian, Carracci, and..." He pointed to the portrait on the wall in the parlor. "And Caravaggio."

Fabiola burst with excitement. "Excellent. Let me meet this man."

"Very well, Signora. I'll enquire, but the artist I'm thinking about has an exceedingly hectic schedule. He paints for both court and Church, as well as the city of Antwerp. He simply may not have the time, but I'll try."

"Thank you, Gillis." She put a hand on his arm. "And I appreciate all the time you've spent trying to satisfy my search for the right artist. What's this man's name?"

"He's called Peter Paul Rubens."

WEDNESDAY, 4 OCTOBER 1944

CHAPTER TWELVE

SOLI'S ARM STILL hurt the next morning. A purplish-green bruise right below the left shoulder was proof of the assault. She stood by the mirror and gently rubbed some lotion on her knee and brushed her hair. Her left temple had a scratch, too. Goodness, even if the thief hadn't gotten anything important from her, she'd been bruised and scraped in several places. Hopefully, her customers wouldn't notice. She styled her hair to the left side to cover the contusion. No need to alarm Nikolai or Heddy. The purse did not contain anything of significance, not a single item to give away who she was or what she did. Thanks to her eidetic memory, she did not keep a notebook of every little detail, and if she did, she'd never carry it around town. She still wondered why she'd been attacked. For all she knew, the thief could have been looking for money or anything of value to sell or trade. Not everything had to be about the resistance work.

She worked on the bills and paperwork between customers and tried not to worry about what had happened. But then Nikolai showed up at the art shop fifteen minutes before closing time.

Nikolai placed a paper bag on the small table and took a step toward Soli. "What on Earth happened to you?" he asked, leaning close to her forehead and gently brushing back the hair she'd styled over the tiny wound.

Having him so close made her stomach flutter. He was newly shaved and smelled of good soap, not the B-soap that reeked of herring oil and mud.

Suddenly, it dawned on her who'd assaulted her the evening before. She opened her eyes wide.

"Sophus Bech."

She almost laughed at the perplexed expression on Nikolai's face, but she caught her breath.

"What about Sophus Bech?" he asked.

"Remember at the auction the other night when you went to help the manager? Well, I spoke with Bech. He said little, but we had a short exchange of words." She gesticulated while she spoke. "Never mind that. The point is, he wore Old Spice."

"And?" Nikolai's face still held a puzzled look. Obviously, he had no idea what she was trying to say.

"The thief who attacked me yesterday left his scent behind. *Old Spice*."

He straightened his back. "Thief? What thief? And you were *attacked*?" His voice became serious.

"Someone pushed me down and stole my purse. I was on my way home from the chiffer club when—"

"When are you girls going to learn not to walk the streets alone late in the evening?"

She put a hand on his shoulder. "But I'm all right, Nikolai, and I hardly had anything in my purse."

"I mean it, Soli. It's not safe."

"I know. But what do you think about the thief wearing the same scent as Sophus Bech?"

Nikolai scratched his chin and smiled. "Very few poor thieves in the capital would wear aftershave. Which brings me to the next question: Do you want to file a complaint?"

"No, I don't think he knows where I live, and as I said, he did not steal anything valuable or incriminating."

"All right, but you watch out if you see him again. I don't want you alone around that man. If I meet him, I'll find out what happened."

Nikolai sat down in her soft, comfortable chair. "I returned to Henry Gran's apartment this morning and searched his desk one more time. I found this scrunched in the back of the top drawer." He handed her a piece of paper.

She took the document and scanned the text. "It's an invitation to an art exhibition at Egil Winther's home on Drammen Road. My goodness, that's an honor."

"Which made me think you may have received the same invitation." He gave her a teasing, sideways look.

Tidiness was not her forte. She flipped her hand at him. "Stop it. If I have one, I'll find it." She ran to her office and returned with the basket she usually used to hold all the incoming mail. *Usually*. Some letters and papers seemed to wander off to other places around the office by themselves. She kneeled by the basket on the floor and started rummaging through the pile.

She leafed through envelopes, documents, and fliers. "Argh, if I have one, it should be here somewhere." She glanced up at him then ducked her head. How embarrassing. She'd unleashed her impatience in front of him.

Nikolai put his feet on an ottoman upholstered with

fabric covered in birds and flowers. He grabbed one of the art history books from the side table, opened it, and chuckled. "I'll just sit here until you find it. Do you have any tea while I'm waiting? A piece of cake perhaps?" He returned the book to the table, leaned back in the chair, and put his hands behind his head.

He was irritatingly charming and impossible to get upset with when he smiled. They'd braved frightening experiences together, and he'd never lost his calm. He managed the double role of holding a high-ranking detective post in the police department subjected to the Nazi regime and being the pillar of strength for Heddy's resistance group. He'd saved them more times than Soli could count.

"What do you know about Egil Winther, Soli?"

She looked up from the mound for a moment to answer. "Mr. Winther is an art connoisseur and has kept his wealth because of his so-called neutrality during the war."

"What does that tell us?"

"He has a talent for finding trendy and also valuable art, and he has a close relationship with both Minister President Vidkun Quisling and the Norwegians who still try to do business without Nazi interference."

"Yes, that's what I've heard, too. He has a foot in both camps and has been successful for years. Something tells me, to do that he's put his weight on the Nazi side."

"I agree." She dug back into the papers. "I've been invited to his house once before, you know. My former employer Mr. Holm and I both attended. It was a dinner and lecture about Far-Eastern painting and calligraphy. Very informative."

She picked an envelope from the pile, tore it open, and

waved the letter in the air. "Ah, here it is." She sat next to him on the armrest and shared the document.

"Let me see." He leaned forward. "Yes, you're hereby invited to an art exhibition at the Winthers' residence on Drammen Road on Saturday, 7 of October 1944. That's only three days away." He lifted his gaze and looked at her with those ocean-blue eyes. "Good thing you found it today then."

She slapped him on the shoulder with the letter. "I know. I'm a mess, but we found it in time. Are you going? I'd feel safer if you were there, too."

"No worries. I'll make sure I'm needed there for security reasons."

She relaxed her shoulders, knowing he'd attend and be across the room when she had to converse with Nazi sympathizers and art connoisseurs, those who had a different agenda than her own. Socializing with such men would be tough enough. Yes, she made her living buying and selling art, but looting and stealing from Jews and other innocent people was corrupt and wrong. If she had lived in olden times, she would have called it her quest, a calling to rescue art out of the wicked, greedy grasps of those who walked over corpses to get their hands on famous and valuable pieces.

Nikolai rose. "Well, I need to get back to work. But before I go, I have something for you." He picked up the paper bag from the table and gave it to Soli.

"What's this?" Opening the bag, she found two sweet raisin and cinnamon rolls with powdered-sugar glaze. She loved sweet baked goods. Her ration card was usually used for other food items; rarely did she buy anything special like this. "Let's share. Do you have time to stay a few more minutes?"

"No, those are for you. I remember you told me how your brother bought you something sweet once a week. Now that he's hiding in Stockholm, you must miss him in more ways than I can imagine. So, as a small token of friendship, you should enjoy those today."

Tears welled up in Soli's eyes, and she gently stroked his arm. "Thank you, Nikolai. Your kind gesture means even more than the treat."

He put his hat back on and tipped it to the side. "You're so welcome. Take care, Soli."

CHAPTER THIRTEEN

SOMEONE RAPPED ON the back door in the early evening. The heavens had opened, and rain poured off the side of the gutter. The drain was crammed with autumn leaves. Soli recognized the special knock. She looked out the window, saw Heddy standing there, and opened the door.

"Hey, Heddy. Come inside. I'm not used to you visiting this time of night."

"I need you to come with me. Are you free right now?"

"Sure. Let me grab my coat and hat." Soli got dressed, put on a pair of boots, and followed Heddy back outside, locking the door behind them.

They walked up the lane next to the art shop and headed for the older part of town beyond the central railway station. Heddy's steps were steadfast and quicker than usual.

Soli did her best to keep up, quickening her pace. "Where are we going, Heddy?"

"Z contacted me. Felix comes to the chiffer group

twice a week after school. He's never missed one of their meetings. Both his mother and his schoolteacher haven't seen him for several days. The boy is missing."

Soli gasped. "That's horrible. He seems like such a nice young man."

"I can't believe it either. First, Henry Gran, and now, Felix. Two of the brightest cryptologists we have. Z needs both of them."

"And we need them to help us find the painting."

They strode past the old Stock Exchange building with its six Dorian pillars up front, then crossed the train station and entered the district that had been the center of Oslo during the Middle Ages.

"Z asked me to go talk with Felix's mother," Heddy said. "I have an address, but I wanted you with me. What if we stumble across something?"

"Does his mother have any idea what he's doing? I mean, his involvement with national secrets. He's still a teenager."

"She must know he's gifted, but I don't think she understands how talented her son is."

Soli agreed. "She can't be told what he does for the resistance. But how did Z recruit Felix?"

"His schoolteacher is involved in the resistance work and recognized Felix's brilliant mind. She told Z, and since then, he's been a great asset for the chiffer group." Heddy turned the next corner and pointed. "It's that building on the right."

Old, two-story wooden row-houses lined the street on both sides.

Heddy paused in front of the entrance to a passageway. "There's another thing. Sophus Bech has been following me around town. I hope my father has kept his promise. I mean, that he hasn't encouraged Bech to contact me."

"How do you know for certain it's him?"

"I'm in the habit of checking every direction when I'm out in the streets. I've seen Bech twice in the last couple of days."

Soli had to mention her encounter with Sophus Bech. At least, her suspicion. She showed Heddy the scrape on her forehead and the bandage on her knee.

Heddy hissed, "I'll get him. He cannot—"

Soli put her hands on Heddy's shoulders. "First things first. All is well with me. Let's go in and find out about Felix."

They climbed the stairs and knocked on the door. A brittle, little woman who looked as if she'd break if you hugged her peeked out at them. Her eyes were red, and her wiry ash-blonde hair unkempt. The overall frowzy appearance took Soli by surprise. Not that Felix gave the impression of a well-to-do upbringing, but he was always neat.

"I'm Miss Hansen, and this is Miss Lund," Heddy said, making up names. "We're from the school district." She sounded convincing and stood straight-backed, maintaining strong eye-contact with the woman.

Felix's mother invited them in and bid them sit. The apartment was one small room, furnished with a trundle-bed that functioned as a sofa during the day and a table for two accompanied by two stools. A narrow kitchen counter with a sink and a cabinet on the wall took up the corner. One window with green curtains had a view to the street.

"My Felix hasn't been home since Friday. He is a good boy, always obedient, and the only activity he has outside of school is a study group he goes to. I've been up every night, waiting for him. Not a word. Nothing. Something's happened. He'd never leave without telling me."

Her frail voice broke as she spoke, revealing the scent of alcohol on her breath. A half-empty bottle sat on the table. She grabbed it and placed it on the floor. She'd probably not be able to buy any such drink at the store. No doubt, she got it from a neighbor or brewed it herself.

"I've stood in the window, hoping he'll come home."

Heddy leaned forward and spoke in a soothing tone. "Have you contacted the police?"

"No, I've been too frightened, but if he doesn't show up, I'll go to the station tomorrow."

Soli said, "We pray for Felix's safe return. You should ask for Inspector Nikolai Lange at the police headquarters at Moller Street 19. He's the best in these matters."

Heddy gave an affirmative nod. The mother seemed satisfied with the suggestion and wrote Nikolai's name on a piece of paper. They bid her goodbye and walked back outside.

The rain had stopped, but their clothes were still damp. They headed back toward the central station at the end of Karl Johan's street.

Heddy hurried, looking down every road they passed. "I'm worried about why Bech follows us around," she said. "Is he onto us? Could it be he knows about our latest operation?"

"I hope not, but we need to find out what he's after. Maybe you should confront him."

Heddy stopped in her tracks. "Soli, are you crazy? Your suggestions are becoming even riskier than mine." Then she smiled and slipped her arm through Soli's and continued walking. "You know, it might be a good idea.

I'll never find out by guessing and imagining what his thoughts are. Besides, I'm tired of changing where I sleep."

Soli gave her a confused stare. "You don't mean you stay someplace new every single night?"

Heddy flipped her hand. "Only these last few days. I used to change once a week."

"I'm sure your friends and relatives are happy to have you visit."

"Could be. Some think I'm too radical for their taste. They're nice, but I have to tell quite a few lies when I'm around them."

Soli had become acclimated to fibbing. Working with the resistance sometimes required not only twisting the truth, but deliberate and straight-faced lying. "What do you tell them?"

Heddy dramatized her voice. "The landlord has kicked me out. I didn't get paid this week. Someone stole my wallet." She lowered her voice. "One time, I came up with a story that the Germans had broken the windows, and the owner needed to replace them."

"Kind of degrading lies, don't you think?"

Heddy laughed. "True. Not very favorable in my case. Yesterday was not a lie, though. I told my aunt I missed her and asked if I could spend the night. It made us both happy."

"You could stay with me."

Heddy squeezed Soli's arm tighter. "That would be the best place to stay, but you need to be our bridge to the art community. That would not work if you house the leader of a resistance group."

They arrived at the marketplace by the church, where they would go their separate ways.

"There's always my secret room in the basement," Soli said and gave Heddy a hug.

"I'm glad there's that choice should we need to use it. For now, we should stay in different places for the safety of both of us." Heddy leaned closer. "Z mentioned she's still not figured out what your fourteen numbers mean."

THURSDAY, 5 OCTOBER 1944

CHAPTER FOURTEEN

SOLI HAD BEEN busy all morning. At one point, five customers explored the showroom at the same time. By afternoon, Soli finally had a quiet moment, which she used to clean and decorate the shop.

She rummaged through the secret room in the basement and exchanged a few of the paintings with ones in the salesroom. The area around the sitting group had been on her mind for a while. She stood on the floor for the longest time. What would people like to see when they sat there, flipping through art books or waiting for a spouse to decide which artwork to buy? She ended up filling a wall with white-matted ink drawings set in shiny black frames. The result was stunning and a welcome variety to the dominating landscape oil paintings in their heavy golden frames.

She sat down in the soft red chair with her hands around a cup of chamomile tea. The hidden painting by Peter Paul Rubens had been in her thoughts all day. Soli had a good idea of the technique he'd used, the brush-strokes and layers of paint, and the typical color palette of the baroque period. But there was also the composition. Even though the portraits varied, the clothing style and surroundings were often similar.

Rubens had painted a vast number of altarpieces during his time in Antwerp. His strong Catholic belief progressed toward the Counter-Reformation, a movement opposing the Reformation that had started with Martin Luther a hundred years earlier. Luther's new religion had spread like wildfire, and from what Soli had studied about the painter Rubens, he'd used his talent to encourage the conservative faith of his forefathers.

Jacob had said the woman in the painting was one of his ancestors. To have a portrait done by Rubens during that time, the model must have come from a wealthy and prominent family. Rubens followed the traditions of Raphael and Michelangelo. He studied the chiaroscuro technique of Caravaggio and had painted for princes and kings, nobility, and ecclesiastical leaders. The Spanish king Philip IV even knighted him in 1631.

Soli was fairly certain who the model in the painting was. Still, she turned over pages in one of her favorite art history encyclopedias and studied the faces of women from the seventeenth century. Behind every face was a story. Soli often woke up thinking her life was difficult, but those women faced the challenge of finding their place in society. Independence and recognition were not for the female race. And what about their liberty? Even during peacetime, they were not free to be their own person.

Something ominous hung in the air whenever she thought of the secret treasure. Clearly, others were after this painting by Rubens. But how much did they know?

Soli was in a riddle contest, battling the enemy by solving brain teasers, deciphering codes to beat her rivals, and dueling her way across the finish line first to win the race. She'd do her best to find out where the Ruber family had hidden the painting and take it to safety, all under the noses of ruthless Nazis who'd kill to succeed. Her task sounded impossible, but she was not about to give up now.

Toward closing time, Birger and Arvid came by the shop. Soli let them in, locked the front entrance, and turned the *closed* sign on the door face out.

"Let's sit in my room," she said. "There's more privacy there."

She'd made her bed that morning. That did not happen every day. The boys sat down on the sofa, and she got a plate of cold potato pancakes and a pitcher with red currant juice from the pantry.

"Tell me all about it," she said, pouring juice into three glasses. "How did you get Jacob safely to the Swedish border?"

Birger grinned as always. Other than Heddy, Birger was the first one Soli had met the day they introduced her to the covert *art club*, a cover name they'd called the branch of the Norwegian resistance who dealt with Nazi looting of art in Norway. Soli's knowledge of art history had caught their interest, and Heddy had recruited her to join them. A newcomer's limited skill with undercover operations had not discouraged the club, and they'd been patient and respectful as she'd learned her way.

Soli knew the feeling of hunger gnawing every day, but for these boys, it had to be worse. That ever-present emptiness they had to experience, stomachs growling, when they ran off on perilous journeys to help others. What good men they were.

Arvid swallowed the last piece of his pancake and helped himself to another.

"We took a train to Espa, north of Oslo. Jacob had new, fake papers, including documentation for living in the eastern zone. There, we met up with a man with a truck. We hopped on the back and hid Jacob under some old hemp sacks. As we approached the bridge across Lake Mjosa, we noticed a German patrol."

Birger leaned forward, his eagerness to continue the story showing in his face. "It shocked us. The Germans have never had soldiers stationed there before. We found out they'd arrived the day before."

Arvid nodded. "Yes, our chauffeur refused to drive on, but our man from the border-help stuck his gun in the driver's side and forced him to step on it."

Birger guffawed. "You should have seen us, Soli. The truck flew through the wooden barricade. Splinters blasted through the air while we held on tight, lying low, and trying to look like potato sacks."

"That's right." Arvid gulped down his juice. "It happened so fast. I mean, the Germans didn't even have time to shoot at us. And we kept on full speed across the bridge, up a hill, and into the woods. There on a dirt road in the middle of the forest, we jumped off the truck and ran eastward as fast as our legs could carry us."

"What about the driver?" Soli asked.

"He returned on his own." Arvid slowed down his speech. "We hope he's all right. Still haven't heard from him, though."

Birger continued. "It was getting dark, and we made

our way to a boat by a small lake in the woods. We rowed to an island and spent the night in a hut out there."

Arvid leaned back in his chair and stretched his long legs. "The next day, Jacob was supposed to cross the border. We walked in the icy rain through swamps, and we balanced on logs across brooks."

Birger made a dramatic expression. "Yeah, I can still hear my shoes go squish, squish, squish—"

"Not that bad. We're used to being wet, aren't we, Birger?" Arvid asked.

Birger nodded. "It took longer than expected, but we got him across eventually. We left to come back here, and somebody else took care of Jacob the remaining few miles."

"We received a message he crossed this morning. He'd slept under a spruce tree the final night when it was too dark to find the way."

Soli stood and poured some water in the empty pitcher. "Well, I'm so grateful he made it across, and you're back here safe and sound. How were you able to cross that bridge the second time?"

"We didn't. We found a farmer who rowed us across a little farther down," Arvid answered.

"So, you just arrived back in Oslo?"

Birger put his hands out and grinned. "Yes, and here we are."

Arvid pushed his plate aside and placed his elbows on the table. "Jacob told us something interesting about the painting we're looking for."

Soli widened her eyes. "He did? Did he remember anything more about where the family has hidden it?"

"Only that he believes it's still in Norway."

"And that eliminates the rest of the world," Birger said, chuckling.

As always, Arvid stayed serious. "He mentioned the old Jewish merchant from the sixteen hundreds had lived in Italy and Malta before moving north to Antwerp. Mobs persecuted the Jews even then. Not just for their faith, but for being prosperous."

"Oh, this is so sad," Soli said. "I've read how Jews were blamed for witchcraft, also, even executed, especially the women. History has not been kind to them."

Birger put a finger up. "Jacob said they'd kept the Italian language for several generations, even after they moved northward through Europe."

"That's interesting," Soli said. "We're finding out about the person in the painting without having seen it."

"And one more thing. They called her Fabiola…Fabiola Ruber."

Soli let out a breath and smiled. "We know Fabiola already—the beautiful model in the Caravaggio painting we hid a while back."

Birger's face lit up, and the corners of his mouth turned upward in a small grin. "That's right. How amazing to find another portrait of the same seventeenth century model."

Soli nodded. "Our goal now is to find the treasured piece of art. Then, we'll keep both of the paintings safe for Jacob and his future family."

"We'll help out, Soli." Birger pushed his chair away and stood. "We need to go now. Thanks for feeding us."

"You're welcome. Come by anytime you're hungry. I'll always share what I have with you."

Birger gave her a hug. "Heddy asked us to invite you to

a meeting at the crypt later tonight. Can you make it in an hour?"

"Yes…but the crypt? Is that safe? The razzia was only a month ago. Why there?"

Birger pulled a sideways grin. "Maybe because it's dangerous, and the Gestapo would not expect us to go back there again."

~ CAPITOLO IV ~
ANTWERP, 1613

FABIOLA SAT IN FRONT of the mirror by her window. The seamstress had brought the new gown the day before, and Nava had laid the clothes ready on the bed. The newly purchased high-heeled shoes with long toes stood paired up on the carpet, as if ready to march off to new adventures.

"Have we not combed your hair long enough, my child?" the old companion asked.

Fabiola stroked the star of David pendant on the necklace she always wore. "Too much is not enough. I want my hair to shine as it did on the last portrait. Everything must be the same. My dogs will accompany us, and—"

Nava rolled her eyes. "The dogs. Oh, my world. I'm getting too old for this."

Fabiola turned and looked at the dear woman. "But, Nava, you love my dogs."

The old lady stroked Fabiola's cheek and smiled. "Yes, I do. They're growing old, just like me." She opened the casket with hair accessories and grabbed a few pins and mother-of-pearl combs.

Fabiola gently pushed them away. "No, my hair should hang down."

Nava protested. "But Fabiola, a married woman of a respectable household cannot wander about the streets of Antwerp with her hair blowing in the breeze like any gypsy."

Fabiola studied the accessories. "Very well. You may do my hair for now, but I'll let it down when we arrive in the artist's studio. Agreed?"

Nava exhaled a brief puff. "You're more stubborn than the mules by the harbor. We'll see when we get there." She dressed Fabiola's hair over a pad, pinned everything in place, then fastened a short string of pearls around her neck.

Fabiola dropped her chin and snickered. Nava would no doubt fall asleep during the session with Signor Rubens. Then Fabiola could let her hair back down for the sitting. The old woman would not last long once she'd had a glass of fruity wine and a comfortable chair with soft cushions to sit in. As a chaperone she was always present. Although Fabiola often smiled, thinking how little the old lady could do should they meet any ruffians along the way.

Fabiola lifted her arms as Nava eased the unfitted coral-colored gown over the bodice and underskirt. In front, the lower part of the satin gown was open and complemented the white material with golden florets of the skirt underneath. The lace-trimmed, three-quarter sleeves were full and loose.

"Lift your arms," Nava said. "Let me tie the ribbon sash around your waist."

Hester entered with Annarosa. The little girl was dressed in a similar yet simpler fashion. The same materials had been used to sew both gowns.

Fabiola put her hands out. "Come, Annarosa. Stand here by the long mirror with me. Do you think we look presentable?"

The little angel laughed and twirled around. Her turn-down collar was trimmed with petit lace like Fabiola's, and the girl had slashed sleeves gathered with a bow above the elbow, allowing the white and gold fabric underneath to show through.

"Are we ready, then?"

Annarosa nodded and skipped with excitement toward the door.

***

Two horse-drawn carriages left the Isaac Ruber home by noon. The first carried women and dogs. Annarosa sat in the middle with her mother on her right-hand side and the nursemaid on the other. On the bench opposite sat Signora Nava. Gillis van Hoye, along with a footman who carried a small trunk of extra clothing, toys, and treats for Annarosa, rode in the second carriage.

Cobblestone lanes rattled the coaches, and the two dogs had difficulty keeping their balance on the floor. The littlest one whined and looked up at Fabiola, but she put her finger out and shushed the small animal. They drove south, turned left on Silversmidstraat, then rounded the corner by the massive city hall that had been built half a century earlier. Fabiola enjoyed this view every time. Statues, columns, and archways adorned the front of the grey stone building that looked out on Grote Markt, the great market square of Antwerp. Circled around the square were guild houses, the headquarter of guilds of craftsmen and merchants. Fabiola's father, brothers, and husband were actively engaged in politics and business around this square. One day, she'd tell Annarosa all about the *gildehuizen* in the heart of town.

"Would it not be easier for Signor Rubens to come to us?" Nava asked. "We're like a procession, driving through the streets."

"I actually prefer to go to his studio. It's satisfactory to be in the creative atmosphere of the artist, to see him in true action, and to feel his inspiration."

"Fabiola, you are a hopeless romantic," Signora Nava said and looked out the window.

"Perhaps, but humor me, Nava. A good portrait is all about sentiment." She turned her head to the nursemaid who was helping Annarosa fix her doll's hair. "Don't you agree?"

Hester opened her eyes wide then lowered her gaze to the carriage floor. "Eh, yes, signora."

The poor girl probably did not dare utter her thoughts. Fabiola realized she hardly ever asked the nursemaid her opinion, something she'd remedy. Hester took care of Fabiola's most precious jewel. Why not get to know her personally?

The carriages passed the Cathedral of Our Lady. The Catholics certainly knew how to build impressive houses of worship. Fabiola had never been inside the Catholic church with its three naves, but she enjoyed the architecture, nonetheless.

They were getting closer now. The streets had grown narrow, and red brick buildings, smaller chapels, apartments, and stores lined both sides. A pothole in the road shook the carriage, and the doll fell to the floor. Annarosa started crying, and Nava quickly picked up the dolly. She comforted the little girl who leaned back in the seat and clutched the doll to her bosom.

The last leg of their journey took them down Joden-straat, where some Jews lived, then they took a sharp left on Wapper. They entered the main gate to the inner court-yard of the master painter's residence. A footman opened the door and led them up the stairs.

They waited a scarce two minutes before a gentleman met them in the upstairs hall. He wore a fitted brown doublet and a lace-edged wing collar that was turned down. His knee-high breeches had a garter with ribbons and rosettes. The man was colorful. His stockings were a bright rust-color and completed his friendly, optimistic appearance.

"Ah, Fabiola Ruber, I presume." He leaned forward and kissed her hand, his long mustache and beard tickling her fingers. "Welcome." Lines formed in the corners of his warm brown eyes.

She smiled and acknowledged his greeting with a slight nod. "May we speak Italian? I have been told you lived there for a while during your studies."

He switched to the Italian language. "Yes, I have spent much time in Italy, journeying throughout the ancient land with my sketchbook in hand. I breathed the atmosphere of the old masters who walked before me." He drew a deep lungful as if to exemplify his sentiment. "I studied them and learned from observing their paintings and sculptures." He turned around, gesticulating as he spoke. "Titian, Veronese, Tintoretto, Carracci, Michelan-gelo, Raphael, Caravaggio. Ah, they are but a few of the talented masters who lived there." He sighed and looked out the window. "All of them dead now, gone to the other side." He straightened his back and smiled. "But we may still enjoy their artwork. That makes this world a better place to be."

Fabiola relished his enthusiasm. Rubens talked about studying ancient art and philology with his brother. The man seemed to meet life through eyes that absorbed every detail, be it dramatic, horrid, or beautiful.

She followed Rubens into the studio, pretending not to notice Nava's frustrated glance when she left her old companion and the others in the hallway. Sketches, brushes, and paints lay on tables. Musical instrument, pots, and various material sat stacked in one corner, and a one-legged table held an open book in the other. Against the left wall stood an armoire with open doors, displaying shelves with tinctures, tin cans full of dried pigment, rags, oils, and color samples.

By a large window stood the biggest easel Fabiola had ever seen. The master was working on a scene. She stepped closer and smiled. The technique she so desired in a painting—the setting of light against dark—was evident.

"You have indeed seen a great deal, Master Rubens."

He nodded. "Yes. I frequently journeyed to Spain on diplomatic assignments for King Philip III and completed commissioned paintings for several churches."

He thought for a moment and put up his finger. "Your padre's assistant Gillis van Hoye has the gift of persuasive oratory. My schedule is often too full to take on single portraits, but he spoke highly of Signora. The citizens of Antwerp have had to get in line behind commissions for the archduke, the town hall, and triptychs and altarpieces for churches and cathedrals."

"I understand you have demanding days, Master Rubens, and I feel privileged to have this appointment with you." She locked her eyes on his. "This portrait is of the utmost importance to me."

The small dog barked in the hallway, and Annarosa started giggling.

He turned. "You brought many people with you. Will there be more than only Signora in the portrait?"

She pulled a slight grin, somewhat embarrassed by the sight and sound in the other room. "I apologize for bringing so many to your studio, but it was necessary. I have a certain portrait in mind, and it involves myself, my young daughter, and the two dogs. The other people are merely to make the visit easier."

Master Rubens smiled. "This is not a problem, Signora. I love children and dogs, but I have a suggestion. We do a sitting today to see how the scene evolves on canvas, and the next time you come alone for close up sketches and details of yourself."

"Agreed." She strolled around the room. The paintings on the wall were magnificent. A few portrait busts and a large sculpture of a man stood next to pots of flowers by the far wall.

"Master Rubens, outside, I noticed the portico...the passage to your garden. How magnificent it is. It reminds me of the triumphal arches of Rome with sculptures and Corinthian and Dorian pillars."

He lit up as she spoke. "You see, Signora, on my last journey to Rome, I started collecting Roman sculptures, reliefs, and even ancient coins." He pointed to the busts in the studio. "Those two are some of the treasures I brought back. When I acquired this estate four years ago, I started renovating. When it is finished, it will be an oasis of remarkable antique art."

He rubbed his hands together. "Now, Signora, let's get to work."

Fabiola sketched what she had in mind on a piece of paper, and the master called on a couple of his assistants to help arrange the scene. They found a high-backed chair for Fabiola, a smaller stool for Annarosa, and draped the background with a silver-colored silk brocade in a fleur-de-lys pattern.

She returned to the hallway. Annarosa was running around, chasing the dogs, with the nursemaid in tow.

Fabiola stopped the red-cheeked Hester in her tracks. "Annarosa will be high and low as usual and is prone to wander off. I worry she may climb onto the windowsill or empty the master's flacons of oils or paints." Fabiola gently patted the wide-eyed nursemaid's hand. "But with you, me, and Signora Nava there to watch the child, we should be able to get through the visit without problems."

"Yes, Signora."

The sitting went better than expected. Rubens had Annarosa sit on the chair, then he made several drafts of her face and head before the little girl fell asleep betwixt two cushions on the floor. Hester sat down for a much-needed rest and was more than pleased when one of Master Rubens's assistants brought a tray with goblets of red wine. Nava drank half a glass and fell asleep, snoring in a comfortable settee. The men discussed politics by the window. Fabiola let her long, dark hair down and sat on the high-backed chair with the large hound by her right knee and the little dog on the lap. Her husband might be staggered when he saw her portrayed like that, but it was a chance she was willing to take.

Fabiola's joy was complete, but would the portrait be what she envisioned? Before leaving, she asked the master to grant her a special request—a few words written in small letters on the backside of the painting.

* * *

Later that evening, Fabiola sat in the parlor. Padre had gone to bed. Even though his coughing was less violent, and the fever had subsided, he still felt the need to sleep longer.

Having met Rubens emboldened Fabiola's hope. Certain she'd found the perfect artist to paint a portrait of her and Annarosa, she reclined in the soft red chair, taking in the painting on the wall that had inspired her visit to Antwerp's master painter that day.

CHAPTER FIFTEEN

OSLO, THURSDAY, 5 OCTOBER 1944

HEDDY SCURRIED DOWN Karl Johan's Street. The stores were closing, and the gigantic clock on top of the corner building behind the *Storting* read five o'clock. She had half an hour before her group came to the meeting at the crypt, so she took time to do something she'd not done in a long while. Slowing down as she turned left on Aker's Street, she lingered in front of several shop windows. She'd not bought any new clothes for years. Not that she had the money to go shopping, but it would be nice to own an extra pair of slacks or a better coat for colder days. She pushed the thought aside. Not now. So many people had less to live on. At least, her aunts and cousins fed her well when she spent the night at their apartments.

She lifted her chin and picked up the pace. She was about to round the corner on the last street that led to the church with the crypt when she spotted Sophus Bech coming out of a cafeteria. She paused for a moment. Should she stop him and talk to him like Soli had suggested, or would it be better if she continued unseen to the crypt to prepare for her meeting with the art club? What good would it do to speak with the man? Why have a conversation with someone who wore a bright-red armband with a black swastika?

The rest of the man looked all right. In fact, he was handsome. A little thin perhaps, but so was she after years of little food. Not that she was interested in Bech's appearance. Sverre was her one and only love, and she longed for him every day.

She let out a long breath. Better find out why Bech had been following her around. She sped up so she could bump into him accidentally, but on purpose.

"Oh, excuse me," Heddy said. Even if the play was horrible, and she'd rather run and hide behind the stage curtain, she acted her part.

"Miss Vengen." He smiled and appeared surprised to see her.

She'd not seen him smile before; it made him look almost friendly. But just barely. She remembered all too well her thoughts of him and who he worked for. She'd better get right to the point.

"I've seen you around town. What do you do when you walk the streets of Oslo?"

Was that straight-forward enough? She could not ask him why he was following her.

He looked into her eyes. "Miss Vengen…may I call you Hedvig? I've been walking the streets in hopes of getting a glimpse of you." He swallowed hard and put his chin forward. "I'm irrevocably infatuated with you."

The answer surprised her even more than the fact that she'd stopped him. And goodness, what big words. What was she to say now? The man was melodramatic, maybe even sensitive to his own feelings. She forced herself to act polite and not blurt out who she was and how impossible a union with him would be. She was not interested on any account.

She gathered her thoughts and said, "Thank you." Cringing, wondering what would come next, she was about to tell him she was late for an appointment when the next shocking sentence came out of his mouth.

"I may work for your father and the Reich, but that doesn't mean I agree with everything they stand for." He adjusted the armband and moved closer to Heddy. "You and I are much alike."

Enough. She did not believe him. Not for a minute. She took a step back. "I apologize, but I'm late for a meeting of my knitting society."

A black car drove up on the next corner, and someone whistled.

"Well, looks like we need to pick this up another time, Hedvig. Duty calls. Goodbye."

She heard his last words as she ran off and hid behind the wooden door of a passageway. Breathing heavily, she put a hand to her chest. The Gestapo drove black cars like that. She was not about to get caught now after four years of fighting them and their likes. Germans or Norwegians, it made no difference. Whoever joined Bech in that car; they were all part of the secret police of Nazi Germany.

Heddy closed the wooden door, ran through the passageway, and hid behind a rabbit cage in the courtyard. She did not dare go out on the street and instead climbed over a fence, ripping a hole in the left thigh of her pants. A narrow strip of garden led to the adjacent building, and a woman opened a window and yelled at her to get away.

"I'm not the enemy," she whispered. She was the only one who heard the words. Or not?

A little white-headed boy in overalls came up to her, a wooden car under his arm. "What's your name?" he asked. "I'm Olav. I'm four."

Such a daring name, the same as the crown prince.

"I'm Heddy."

Did she dare ask the little man a favor? "Olav, do you want to earn some money?"

"How much?" he asked, his innocent blue eyes shining with determination.

Surprised at his response, she stifled a laugh. "Well, Olav, can you crawl under the gap in the fence there, run like the wind down the passageway, and look out the door back there to see if a big, black car is still on the corner?"

He nodded and made his way as fast as his little legs could carry him. Within seconds he returned, holding out his hand.

"Answer first," Heddy said.

The boy replied without hesitation. "I looked both ways, but there were no cars at all out there. But I did see a bicycle. It was black."

"Good boy." She placed a five øre copper coin in his hand.

The boy made a fist around the money and ran off.

Should she go back out there? Could they be hiding somewhere, ready to arrest her as she hit the street?

She waited another twenty minutes then climbed back across the fence. She slunk through the passageway. Up the street, a group of soldiers waited in line for the bar to open. Heddy hurried down the opposite way, pretending not to hear the whistles and remarks from the soldiers.

* * *

Soli cut across the marketplace by Our Savior's Church and spotted Rolf enter the gate on the right side of the tall stone building that had been a place of worship for two hundred and fifty years. She stopped to let a tram pass, crossed the street, and waded through the leaves to the entrance of the crypt. Birger and Arvid sat on the steps. They stood as she approached.

Turning the key in the lock of the massive wooden door, Rolf nodded to Soli. "Hello. Glad you could make it."

"Are you sure this is safe?" Soli walked closer.

"Nothing's ever sure these days, but I spoke with the minister and asked him if we could have the crypt for an hour or two. He said he'd keep an eye out for unwanted visitors while we were here."

Rolf swung the door open and turned the light switch on the wall inside the door. "I thought Heddy would be here already."

They descended a stairwell into the dimly lit but spacious room under the church. Old coffins and gravestones sat amid pillars under the vaulted ceiling, the sarcophagi for members of some of the richest families in Oslo during the last few centuries.

"Where is she?" Arvid said and sat down on a chair by the table to the left. "Heddy's always here before we arrive."

Rolf shrugged. "No idea. We'll wait a few minutes before we start. She'll show up before long."

Even Birger had a long face and no smile or teasing look in his eyes.

Rolf put a hand on the young man's shoulder. "Let's

not worry. She could be held up by something insignificant."

Small talk was awkward. Soli delivered a small lecture about Peter Paul Rubens. The boys were interested and intrigued, as always, but Rolf checked his wristwatch more than normal. Birger and Arvid kept looking toward the door. Where was she? An hour had passed. What if something bad had happened to Heddy? Had someone discovered what she was involved with?

"That's it!" Arvid stood, his voice resolute. "I'm going out to search for her."

"I'll come with you." Birger looked thin and frail compared to Arvid's towering stature, but the two made an excellent team.

The sound of a key turning in the lock startled everyone. Rolf put a finger on his lips. They all froze until they saw Heddy come down into the light. Birger ran forward and threw his arms around her.

"Thank you, Birger. I'm glad to see you, too." Heddy's face was pale and her eyes red.

Soli hugged her. "Come, sit. You look like you've seen a ghost."

Rolf pulled out a chair. "You had us worried. What happened?"

Heddy sat down and placed her hands on the table. "I bumped into Sophus Bech on the corner of Grensen and Aker's Street."

"How do you know he didn't follow you here?" Birger asked, leaning against a stone pillar.

"He didn't; I'm sure, but I was scared his friends noticed me."

"Who?" Rolf leaned forward, locking his eyes on her with an intense stare.

"A black car came to pick him up."

"Oh, no." Rolf leaned back and pulled his fingers through his dark hair. "You don't want the Gestapo on your tail."

Arvid sat down next to Heddy. "Did they see you?"

"No, Bech left with them after we spoke. Said he had an important assignment. I dodged behind a building as soon as the car drove up and waited until they were long gone before I risked showing myself back on the street."

Rolf walked around the table and patted Heddy's shoulder. He pulled a bottle of water out of his bag and placed it in front of her. She gave him a grateful glance and drank half of his drink. Their courageous leader had been afraid, no question about it.

Heddy handed the bottle back to Rolf. "I mean, one minute he tries to convince me he's not a Nazi, and the next he's all excited to jump into a car and run off to a so-called assignment with them...the enemy. Is it just me, or is that man difficult to read?"

Rolf scowled. "He's either intentionally ambiguous or stupid. I don't think he means to speak with a double tongue, but he should be careful."

"But it's still interesting how he comes across with two opposite meanings," Arvid said. "We should not underestimate either position."

No one questioned Heddy. Time and again, she'd proven how wise her judgement was. Soli could tell the team respected Heddy's sound guidance. But their worried faces showed they no doubt thought the same thing Soli did. What had the Gestapo seen?

Heddy grabbed a roll on the table and took a bite. "Confusing, isn't it? Well, I don't trust him."

"Did you see who else was in the car?"

"No, I didn't wait around long enough. It could have been my father or even Heinz Walter. I didn't want any of them to notice me. I probably stayed hidden longer than I had to, but I was petrified they'd return and arrest me, and I'd put all of you in danger."

"Oh, Heddy. We're fine," Soli said. "In my opinion, one vital piece of information has come out of this experience."

They all stared at her.

"I don't think Sophus Bech understands the work you do. Don't you think that black car would have chased you down if he did?"

"Well put, Soli." Rolf sat back down. "Now, let's talk about Felix and Henry Gran. Still no news about them?"

Birger stepped up to the table. "We could send a message to Grini."

Heddy looked up at him. "That's a grand plan, Birger. If either of them have been arrested and placed in the detention camp at Grini, our guys in there should be able to tell us."

"How do you get a message through to the prisoners?" Soli asked.

Heddy explained. "Some bakeries in town make bread for the inmates at Grini. They smuggle letters so we can communicate with our men who are locked up. We also bring word to their families they are alive."

Birger sighed. No smile lit up his friendly, freckled face. "I hope I never go back there."

Rolf folded his arms. "What other options do we have? Who do we think ransacked Henry Gran's apartment, and where did they take him?"

"If the German police get the notion either Gran or

Felix have vital information, they'll stop at nothing to make them reveal their secrets," Heddy said.

Birger cleared his throat. "I was interrogated at Grini. I didn't tell them anything, Heddy. I swear, I didn't."

Heddy put her arm around his shoulders. "I know, Birger. And you were one of the lucky ones to be set free."

Birger looked down and nodded.

"Gran and Felix could've been shot," Arvid said.

Heddy cleared her throat and straightened up. "Let's be positive. What have we missed?"

Soli kept thinking about Henry Gran's apartment. Something was not right there. What had happened the day Gran had disappeared? "I'll ask Nikolai if we can go back to Gran's apartment."

Heddy clapped her hands. "Good. Let's all keep our eyes and ears open."

* * *

A short while later, after saying goodbye to the boys, Heddy asked if Soli had a minute.

"Yes, of course. Always."

"He said he was in love with me." Heddy's expression showed disgust and worry at the same time.

"It was risky meeting him. I'm sorry I encouraged you to talk with him."

Heddy let out a lengthy, exasperated breath. "Well, I said very little. But like you said, now we know a little more about him."

"Even if he likes you, it doesn't mean he's not lying about being against the Nazi regime. He could have said that to get close to you."

Heddy put her hand on her hip. "Some women do

anything to obtain the information they want." She looked mutinous. "I may throw myself into dangerous situations more often than not, but I'd never go there. I'd never lose my dignity and self-respect. I also have Sverre to think about. He's everything to me."

Soli smiled and stroked Heddy's cheek. "That's one more good thing we have in common."

FRIDAY, 6 OCTOBER 1944

CHAPTER SIXTEEN

FLUFFY WHITE CLOUDS were in the distance as the sun came up over Oslo. Soli pulled the blinds aside and let the first rays of sunshine into the room. A dove cooed from the fence in the back yard. Everything seemed tranquil until Soli remembered. There was a war outside her home—a dreadful, omnivorous state of fear and terror—but she refused to stay in that horrible turmoil. The bird cleaned its wings and cooed a little more. The dew on the autumn leaves glistened in the morning light. There had to be room for hope and a promise of better days.

Soli sat down by the window to mend Heddy's torn black pants. Her friend had come by very early, confessing she'd never held a needle and thread in her fingers. Heddy appeared exhausted and had dark rings under her eyes. Soli had ordered her to sleep.

Heddy lay curled up under the covers on the sofa bed. Soli would fry the three eggs she'd received from a customer the day before and serve them with half a loaf of bread. She'd not take no for an answer and allow Heddy to run off as soon as she woke up.

By a quarter to nine, the sleeping beauty had still not stirred. Soli fried the eggs and put a plate on the table, along with a note telling Heddy not to leave until she'd eaten her breakfast.

Fifteen minutes later, Soli opened the shop and received the first customer of the day. An older woman with a small dog in her arms needed a book about Impressionism. The conversation was entertaining as the woman had an expert knowledge of the modern movement. Claude Monet was her favorite artist of the period, and she even quoted him, saying, "What I like most of all in London is the fog." The old lady chuckled and said Monet would have loved Oslo these last few weeks. "But not today," she said. "Today the sun is out, and I couldn't be more pleased. I'll go home and enjoy this book."

To have a positive attitude like that was a gift. The challenges and fears the last four years had subdued Soli's natural-born optimism. She pledged not to let war destroy her. Pleasant words like hope and buoyancy should be ingrained in her heart.

She went back to check on Heddy and found the pants gone, the sofa-bed made up, the plate empty, and the words *thank you* written in large, bold letters at the end of Soli's note. At least, Heddy had rested and could start the day with a full stomach.

* * *

Rolf came by the art shop in the afternoon, but there was still no news about Felix or Henry Gran. Soli had sent a message with an errand boy to Nikolai, asking him to meet her at Gran's apartment after she'd closed up the store.

A thought bothered her. Why did Hitler have such hatred of the Jewish people? Even in her country, far in the north, the leaders adhered to the Führer's admonition to remove Jews from society. Where had Leon Ruber and his family and friends been taken? Why had none of them returned?

Soli met Nikolai on Gran's street after work.

"I've been thinking," she said as she followed him up the stairs to the second floor.

Before she continued, Nikolai turned, and his smile caught her off guard.

"I can't wait to hear. Your thoughts are in a place beyond mine. Every detective should have a Soli Hansen on their team."

Not sure how to answer, she lowered her gaze.

The neighbor woman opened her door a crack, leaving the chain on. She peeked out through the narrow space, her eyes wide with fearful curiosity.

Nikolai took a step closer and showed his badge. "Police business. We'll be gone in a few minutes."

The woman nodded and disappeared back into her cave.

Soli followed him inside Gran's apartment. Nikolai walked about the flat, dodging the mess on the floor as he put a chair in place by the table and straightened a lampshade.

"Let's hear what you've been contemplating, Soli."

She placed herself in the middle of the living room. "Look at the scuff marks on the floor."

He came and stood next to her. "Yes, they go from here

to…" He turned toward the entrance. "And to the door over there. Someone dragged Gran and—"

"You know what this means, don't you?" Excited to tell him about her discovery, she did not wait for him to finish.

Nikolai gave her a blank stare and scratched his head. If it had not been for her eagerness to explain, she would have laughed. Instead, she kept a straight face and said, "Henry Gran is not the one who was hauled out of this apartment."

"How do you figure that?"

She pulled a grin. "The old man is not the victim here. Let me describe what I mean."

Nikolai put his hands up. "Please do."

"First, we've concluded no one broke in. The culprit either had a key or was let into the apartment." She walked to the table. "There are two wine glasses on this table." She placed her thumb and forefinger at the base of one of the crystal goblets and slid it in circles on the table. The small amount of liquid left in the glass swirled around. "Gran had a drink with his visitor. Recently. The last drops of wine have not dried in the goblet's bottom. Ergo, they were friendly."

"All right. I agree with you on that, but what about the scuff marks? Why could the two not have had a skirmish, and the visitor knocked Gran unconscious or even killed him?"

"Because it was Felix who was dragged across the floor."

"The missing boy from the chiffer group? His mother came by my office two days ago. Said it was not like her son to be gone overnight without telling her. I've had men out looking for him, but we have made no progress finding him. He could be anywhere and nowhere." Nikolai directed an index finger at Soli. "You're keeping me busy, young lady."

She sighed. "I know. I don't mean to. We just have to find him. Now, check those scuff marks again." She kneeled and pointed to the two stripes along the floor. "It seems as if he was dragged through the room here. See how different the two lines are? The left abrades are dark—"

"Black leather soles caused them. But the lines on the right side are not the same, less visible and brown." He scratched his head. "I'm sure you can explain, Soli."

"When I saw Felix, I noticed how poorly he was dressed. Especially his brown leather shoes. The soles were worn down, and the right shoe had hardly any heel left."

"Ah, clever. That explains the two different marks. But why would Felix come here? Were he and Henry Gran friends?"

"No, I think his visit had to do with something they'd discovered, or rather what Gran had found out." She walked down the hallway and opened the front door. "Come, Nikolai. There's more."

"Yes, miss."

She stepped outside and picked up a chewing gum wrapper. "Felix chews gum all the time. Paper wrappers with this same brand were on the floor by his chair in the chiffer group room."

"I see. Very observant." He rushed to the staircase. "The scuff marks are less noticeable here but seem to continue this way."

Soli touched his shoulder. "Who do you think did this to Felix?"

Nikolai shrugged. "I don't know. Let's hope he's still alive."

"I'm praying he is. He seems like a good young man. His exceptional talent brought him to the chiffer group, and he doesn't deserve to be hurt, whatever's happened."

CHAPTER SEVENTEEN

SOLI CLOSED THE DOOR and followed Nikolai down the stairs, past the ground entrance, and into the basement.

He lit a match to see the scuff marks better. "They seem to end about here," he said, facing a door.

Soli grabbed the handle. "It's locked. In my uncle's apartment building, the key to the basement is on a nail above the door." She looked around for the key but came back and shook her head. "Nothing."

Nikolai stretched and felt the frame above the entrance. "Not here, either. But wait a minute. Sometimes, these basement locks use a master key. Let's try mine." He retrieved a key from his pocket, pushed it into the keyhole, and turned it. Nikolai gave Soli a nod and shoved the door open.

Paralyzed, Soli stood motionless as if something dreadful in the room had clutched her body. Would they find Felix alive? Was he even there anymore?

Nikolai nudged her and whispered, "Are you doing all right?"

She nodded and followed him into the murky chamber. A tiny window allowed a small beam from the streetlamp outside but not enough to see the interior. Soli stroked her hand on the wall next to the door and found a switch. The glass ceiling lamp was dirty. It took a minute before Soli's eyes adjusted to the dim light. She tripped over an empty sack on the floor, and Nikolai helped her back up.

"This is the storage space for the residents of the apartments." He spoke low, pointing around. "Look, there are skis, shovels, even ice skates hung up on nails on the wall."

They made their way around boxes and old suitcases. Nikolai lit another match and held it close to the floor. "There are some faint grazes right here." He lifted his head and pointed. "They go in that direction."

Soli followed on tiptoe, then she grabbed his arm. "I hear something."

Whimpering groans came from the back. Nikolai lifted a stack of boxes out of the way, and Soli helped move shovels and rakes. The smell was intolerable. A waste bucket sat next to a barrel, and in the other corner sat Felix.

Soli jumped forward and dropped to the floor in front of the boy. "Are you all right?"

He nodded. The dry blood from the scratch on his forehead looked stark against his ghostly skin, and one eye was black. Other than that, he seemed unharmed. With empty eyes, he stared at Nikolai.

"Felix, this is Inspector Lange. He's been looking for you. You can trust him."

"Let's get these off." Nikolai pulled a knife out of his pocket and cut the cords around Felix's wrists and ankles.

The young man rubbed the joints where the tight ropes had bound him. "Thank you. I've never been so frightened in my life. I've yelled and shouted, but no one heard me."

"Thank goodness, you're alive. We've been worried," Soli said.

Felix straightened his back and rolled his shoulders. The chafed skin on his left wrist and hand were proof he'd tried to get the ropes off.

Nikolai handed him a handkerchief from his pocket. "Here, tie that on your hand. It looks painful." He squatted next to the boy. "What were you doing in Henry Gran's apartment?"

Felix tied the cloth around his fingers and rested the hand in his lap.

"One evening at the chiffer group, I noticed Mr. Gran hid some of his notes, as well as intelligence documents, in his leather bag. I peeked when he wasn't looking." Felix swallowed hard. "The old man went home that night with those papers. I knew he was working as a double. So, I went to his apartment to confront him, to ask him what was going on, but Mr. Gran became enraged. I thought about screaming for help, but then I thought I could talk some sense into him. He responded by knocking me down. When I awoke, I was down here with a horrible headache."

Soli gawked. "I can't believe he's collaborating with the Germans. You could have been in worse danger had they come for you." She stretched out her hand and helped Felix up. "We must get you out of here."

Nikolai stepped closer. "One moment, Soli. Once we're

out on the street, we have to act normal." He turned to Felix. "You've just faced a murderer. What more can you tell us?"

Felix looked appalled. "Mr. Gran left me here alone for days with only some water and a little food. He's dishonest and greedy, but a murderer?"

"He may not have had the guts to commit homicide, but he left you hidden here in the basement." Nikolai picked up an empty water container and a torn paper wrapper. "When did you run out of food and drink?"

"Only this morning."

"Well, if Soli had not suspected a connection between you and Gran, who knows how much longer you'd have lasted." Nikolai placed the knife in his pocket. "I gather you were not the one who had a glass of wine with Henry Gran earlier. Did you see anyone? It may be important to the investigation."

Felix coughed. "Excuse me. My throat is dry."

Soli dug in her pocket, found a piece of chocolate, and handed it to Felix. "You must be famished. Just a few more questions and we'll be on our way."

Felix shoved the chocolate into his mouth. "Mr. Gran had someone in his apartment before I came, but the man left as I was walking up the stairs."

Nikolai rubbed his chin and leaned forward. "Did this person see you?"

Felix shook his head. "I held my head low. My sixpence covered my face. But I got a look at him from the window on the landing when he walked away. The fellow was not too old, tall, and he wore a fine suit, not the cheap kind."

"Anything else?" Nikolai asked. "I know you're tired, but everything helps."

Felix coughed and wiped his nose on his sleeve. "He

had a Nazi band on his arm and dragged his leg when he walked. Oh, and he wore too much aftershave, stinking up the stairwell as he passed."

Sophus Bech. Soli caught Nikolai looking her way. No doubt, he had the same thought. It had to be Bech, but why had he visited Henry Gran?

From what Soli could see in the apartment, Gran had an exceptional interest in art history. The news of his knowledge and expertise must have reached the Nazi art community.

The young man was shaking now. Soli recognized the look on his face. That crippling fear that freezes the muscles and causes the heart to beat against the chest. Battling a powerful enemy was no game.

She leaned forward and took hold of his trembling hands to calm him. "There's something else I need to know. It could be important. Are you up to it?"

Felix nodded.

"The apartment was a mess when we got there. Was it like that when you were there?" she asked.

"No, not at all. Mr. Gran is very neat."

Soli gave Nikolai a quick glance then asked, "Did he say anything to help us understand why someone was after him?"

Felix thought for a moment. "Before he knocked me out, Mr. Gran said he needed to get rid of me then disappear for a while. Maybe working with two opposite parties became too much for him?"

"Good. I believe you're on to something very vital there," Nikolai said.

At first glance, anyone would think Felix a typical young man, but his gaze was more concentrated than most. Even in this frail state, his mind probably spun with ciphers and letters, decrypting codes and riddles.

She took a scrap of paper and a pencil out of her pocket and wrote the fourteen numbers. "Here, Felix. You need to burn this note after you've checked it out."

He pushed the blond bangs away from his blue eyes and took the note. "What is it?"

"I need your help to figure out what the numbers mean."

His eyebrows rose. "Where did you find it? Is this the sum of something, the quantity of a shipment, or what?"

Soli shrugged. "We're hoping you can tell us."

"I know what it means," he said and winked. "It's the number of times the Germans have offended us, not counting how often they've broken our laws."

Bless his heart. A little humor no doubt rescued him from heavy responsibility time and again. Soli could not explain where she'd found the numbers. Felix had enough secrecy on his plate already. They should spare him the danger of involving him any further.

"I'll do my best, Soli." He looked at Nikolai. "Can we go now? I'm really tired."

Nikolai patted his shoulder. "Of course. Thank you for answering our many questions."

Nikolai helped Felix through the rubble in the storage room, and with an arm around the young man's waist, he hauled him up the stairs and out to the street. Soli locked the basement door and followed them to the car.

"You can stay with me for a while if you need to," Soli said. "I have an extra room."

Felix shook his head. "I need to hurry back to my mother. She must be worried about me." His legs failed him, and he collapsed on the ground.

Nikolai reached out to help him up. "I'll take you home. But, Felix, you'll have to come up with a story for your mother. It's best not to speak of this to anyone."

SATURDAY, 7 OCTOBER 1944

CHAPTER EIGHTEEN

SOLI WAS STILL asleep when Heddy came knocking on the back door. Soli stumbled out of bed and turned the key in the lock. Like a cat, her friend slipped into the room, noiseless and nimble. Heddy could sneak in anywhere without being observed.

"I've just seen Nikolai and heard all about how you solved the case and found Felix. Bravo. You're not only a wonderful art dealer, you are a crime solver, as well!"

"I wouldn't say that. We still don't know where Henry Gran is. Besides, Nikolai guided me. He makes it seem easy."

Yes, Nikolai was growing on her. It was more than his dreamy, marine-colored eyes or the dimple in his chin. The man was kind and thoughtful, and she always felt she could be herself around him.

Heddy cleared her voice. "Am I to understand you and our detective friend—?"

Soli shook her head. "No, no. He doesn't know. I just...yes, I like him...a lot."

"He's a good man, Soli."

"He is." She rolled her eyes and smiled. She'd just realized a few days ago how much she enjoyed Nikolai's company, and already she'd blurted out the news to someone else. So much was going on. It was a difficult time to fall in love. But she'd fallen—off a cliff and into the unknown.

Soli breathed a sigh of relief and smiled at Heddy. "I couldn't have kept it from you much longer."

"Probably not," Heddy said and winked. "But I'm glad you told me."

Soli grabbed a piece of paper on the table. "Look, I forgot to tell you. I've received an invitation to an art exhibition."

"Who's inviting? Is it the same party Nikolai is attending today?"

"Yes. Here, you can read it." Soli handed Heddy the letter.

Heddy read aloud. "A Soiree at Drammen Road." She waved the paper in front of Soli. "Yes, that's the one. You must go."

"You know I cannot stand large social gatherings and nonsensical conversations, but Nikolai will be there."

"Yes, and this is an art event, Soli. I would guess all the significant art dealers in Oslo will be there. You know many of them already. Besides, you might pick up some useful information."

Tears stung behind Soli's eyes, and her mother's words to her as a child rang in her ears *Sometimes, you must do things you don't want to do.*

Oh, Mor, how often have I kept going because of your wise words? Talking to strangers, being in crowds—was Soli getting any better at those things? Working undercover with Heddy and her art club took all the courage she could muster...courage she always seemed to be lacking.

Heddy wiped away a tear that had escaped and rolled down Soli's cheek. "You and art...it's an exceptional symbiosis. The art world needs someone who does not rescue the treasures unto themselves and whose primary objective is not greed. You've found your gift, Soli...or maybe it found you."

"Thank you, Heddy. I'll go. I just need to vent my discomfort now and then. It seems like every day has bumpy roads and new, unnerving challenges. Will we ever have a break?"

"Not as long as there's a war to win."

* * *

A rushing wind smelling of salt and fish had come ashore and ruffled the Nazi banner on the front of the town hall. The building was still under construction, and only part of it was used for offices. Soli crossed the square and breathed the freshness of the air. It had the scent of being home. Out on the Oslo fiord, a ship cut the waves, ferrying people back and forth to the many islands in the bay.

Soli wore a pair of elegant, high-heeled red shoes. No fish-skin pumps today. A touch of class was necessary for an evening at Mr. Winther's residence. She'd planned enough time to get there in heels. The walk was more than half an hour and the weather unpredictable. Her flat, brown shoes would have been a more comfortable choice.

The shoes matched her rosy-red dress suit with its v-neckline and button-down front. Since she'd given away her shoulder bag to Jacob, and Sophus Bech had stolen her small purse, she'd borrowed a black clutch from Heddy. Her hair was pinned back, and all she needed now was the confidence to go with the outfit.

She passed the art gallery on Bygoy Allée where she'd attended the auction earlier in the week and continued through Frogner with its villas and older apartment buildings dating to the nineteenth century.

She slowed down as she approached Mr. Winther's villa. The apricot-pastel brick building with its carved arched front door looked impressive. Stone columns on either side of the gate had lit torches attached to the top. She was lucky to be part of the art community and receive an invitation to such a lavish happening. On the other hand, she would be more than happy to turn around and go back home. But as Heddy had said, maybe something important would come out of observing the people who came tonight.

As she'd expected, the event attracted all kinds. A group of men in Gestapo uniforms and sharp-edged hats stood on the balcony on the second floor, smoking. The French doors were wide open, and the sound of talking and the clinking of glasses floated into the street. Colleagues she'd met before walked ahead of her up the stone path. Prominent citizens, whose loyalty wavered, depending on which side would best secure their wealth and interest, arrived in cars and by horse and buggy. Few survived a war situation, especially in an enemy-occupied country, with their riches intact.

She made her way past servants with trays. Groups of two and three men in suits or uniforms lingered near the entrance, deep in conversation. Laughter and music rang from the grand hall straight ahead. Soli entered, stretching her neck to see if she could find a friendly face to avoid unnecessary new introductions.

Double doors led into another salon. Framed water-color paintings in different sizes decorated the room. The pictures depicting typical Norwegian scenery sat on easels, chairs, leaned up against heavy candlesticks on the table, and were even propped up against books in the bookcase.

An elegant woman wearing a long black silk gown, a stola draped around her neck, approached Soli. Her silver hair was up, and glittery earrings dangled close to her shoulders.

"Mrs. Winther." Soli took the elegant woman's outstretched hand and gave a quick curtsy.

"Miss Hansen, you cannot believe how pleased I am to see you here. I was hoping you'd come." She flipped her hand. "Just look at this...men everywhere. I told my husband to invite the wives, but he refused. But you, my dear, as the only female art dealer in town, are a welcome sight." She looked Soli up and down. "I adore that dress. The color is superb on you."

"Thank you." Short for words, Soli tried to come up with something sensible to say. She did not want to discuss the weather, so she pointed to the aquarelles. "These are new to me. Can you tell me about them?"

Mrs. Winther hooked her arm around Soli's and started a tour of the room. "This, my dear, is a special collection. A handful of German soldiers who are stationed here painted these."

She must have noticed Soli's baffled expression. "It should not surprise you, dear. Even the Führer has artistic talent. He used to paint, you know, but I expect he's much too busy nowadays." Mrs. Winther hummed a small giggle, as if she found her own story amusing but had not laughed for a long time. She continued strolling about the room with Soli in tow. "Hitler appreciates creativity. What do you think? Is this art worth having on your wall?"

They paint as if they own our country, as if they accentuate their occupation by putting it on canvas. No, Soli would never have one on her wall, no matter how lovely the water-colors were. The paintings depicted the four seasons, wintry landscapes, rugged mountains diving into fiords, birches in golden colors, and heather-covered moors. She could never appreciate the beauty, knowing the background of the project.

Afraid she'd reveal her personal disgust with the exhibition, Soli said, "I'm surprised the soldiers have time to paint. They should spend their days here painting."

Once again, Mrs. Winther sounded like she choked on a giggle. "Soli. Soli...you're so right. We'd not be in this mess had the soldiers developed their talents instead of learning how to fight." She lifted her chin and waved to an older man on the other side of the room. "Excuse me, dear. I need to greet our neighbor." The silken gown swooshed as she strolled across the floor.

Soli had the impression the woman lived a life without expressive joy, longing for a friend to share her thoughts with. Growing up without a close girlfriend, Soli hadn't known what she lacked. Today, she couldn't imagine not having Heddy around...a confidant with whom Soli could share everything. Even if she hoped to have a close relationship with Nikolai one day, Soli believed women needed women.

Someone clapped their hands, demanding attention in the grand hall. Mrs. Winter rustled in behind Soli and tapped her on the shoulder.

"Don't you want to step closer? Here in the back by the door is too far away to hear."

Soli smiled. "I can hear from here. Thank you, though."

"All right. I need to go stand by my husband."

Soli counted about thirty men in the room. Mr. Winther stood behind a wooden lectern. He held his hands on the sides of a pulpit.

"Honored guests, I am pleased to present an art aficionado, an excellent judge of fine painting, drawing, architecture, and sculpture. This man knows his history, and I'm sure we can learn a great deal when he now gives us a small portion of his learning. I give you Henry Gran."

Shocked that Gran was there, Soli almost jumped when Nikolai eased in to stand behind her. He nudged her arm. Into the room came Henry Gran, straight-backed and serious. Sophus Bech escorted Gran on one side, and an older man walked on the other.

Soli turned halfway to Nikolai. "Is that—?"

He nodded. "Yes. Heddy's father…"

The two men followed Gran up to the lectern as if they were delivering a parcel there.

Gran stood for a moment, looking out on the crowd, then he pulled out some notes from his inside pocket and started speaking.

Oh, had the circumstances been different. The man was brilliant. He spoke of major influences in art history and recurring subjects in paintings. Soli reveled in hearing about terms and styles, but this was not the time and place to go deep into the topics she loved so dearly.

As Gran made his end remarks, an officer in an immaculate German uniform turned his head to say something to another standing beside him. Baffled, Soli studied his profile. Could it be? It was. She turned and hurried out into the hallway.

There was no doubt about it. The infamous Lieutenant Colonel Heinz Walter was still in the country, no doubt up to wreaking havoc and destruction. Hands shaking, she left without thanking Mrs. Winther. Nikolai came after her, closing the door behind him to the grand hall.

"What's wrong, Soli?" He took hold of her hands.

"Heinz Walter was there. I saw him. He'd kill to find out what I know."

Nikolai nodded. "Yes. It's best you don't meet him right now."

They heard a noise from the grand hall. He checked to make sure no one came out to the entry.

"Henry Gran was not there of his own choice," Nikolai whispered. "The man looked petrified."

"He seemed to forget where he was for a while when he dove into his lecture."

"True. Gran is just a small fish in a sea of sharks. They want his expertise and knowledge. He fell for their enticing prospects, but they'll swallow him whole when they don't need him anymore. Gran will soon find out what little worth the Reich places on people, even their own."

Nikolai looked out the window by the front door and waved for her to come closer. "Look, Soli. My men are out there with Gran. We're taking him under arrest."

Surprised, Soli narrowed her eyes. "Here? Now?"

He nodded. "It's the right thing to do, but I've asked my guys to do it quietly. We don't want to cause a scene here. And with many Nazis working at the police station there's no way I can bring him in for handing over information to the Germans. But I can arrest Gran for abducting Felix. He won't get away with that."

"I'm confused," Soli said. "Will Bech and Vengen let the police take him away?"

"Well, fortunately, I trust my men. Earlier today, after we'd heard Gran was giving a speech here, my officers had a good talk with Bech. They pulled all the pro-Nazi strings they could, pretended to support their cause, and let Bech know Gran had to be brought in and questioned for abducting a young man. Bech didn't want to be involved and agreed to quietly take Gran out the back door after the presentation."

"And Heddy's father?"

"Bech mentioned he and Vengen didn't need Gran anymore. The old man had served his purpose." Nikolai let out a long breath. "I hope we can get some information out of him, but who knows what he's already told the enemy?"

Soli's stomach was in knots. "I don't like the sound of this."

"I know. Come, Soli. Let's go out and talk with Gran." Nikolai gently took hold of her arm and led the way out the main gate.

"Can I ask him about the painting?" Soli whispered.

Nikolai shook his head. "Let's wait to see what he says first."

The police car was parked in the shadows of a large oak, and the old man stood pale faced, an officer on either side holding his arms.

"Henry Gran, my name is Inspector Lange. I've been looking for you." Nikolai's tone was strict and forward. "It was quite a surprise to see you here this evening. Can you believe it? We've been sincerely worried about what happened to you."

Gran's head hung low. "I've made some foolish choices."

Nikolai nodded. "And, might I add, dangerous ones."

"I see that now, but you have to understand. They forced me to give the Germans that information." Gran looked up, his eyes red. "I had no choice. They were going to kill me."

Soli could not help herself and blurted out, "Why haven't you been back to your apartment? You left everything, making the police believe you were abducted or even killed."

"I was ashamed. How would you feel if you realized you'd betrayed your country? I'd planned to run away when they came and forcefully dragged me out of my home."

"Who?" Nikolai asked.

Gran did not answer.

Soli still did not trust the man and left out the information that someone had ransacked his apartment. "If you're innocent, then why did you treat Felix the way you did? You hit him over the head and tied him up in the basement."

Nikolai took a step closer to Gran and put a finger up in his face. "If Soli had not figured out where young Felix was, he could have died."

Gran lowered his head and said with a quaver in his voice, "I only wanted to protect the lad. He's smart, and I should have expected he'd figure out my involvement with the enemy. So, I did the thing that came up first in my mind. I hid him so the Germans wouldn't find him."

"Which Germans? Who talked you into handing over information?"

Gran squirmed. "I cannot..."

"You can and you will."

Nikolai folded his arms and kept strict eye contact with Gran, but the old man pursed his lips and looked the other way.

"Well, this is what we'll do." Nikolai rubbed his chin. "I can't arrest you for aiding the Germans. Just think about the clientele here this evening. But my men will take you in for abducting and hurting Felix. You'll be questioned at the police station at Moller Street 19, and circumstantial evidence could be beneficial if you speak the truth. You claim it was not your will to collaborate with both sides. Go willingly now, and we'll take all that's happened into consideration. But I tell you, Gran, if you keep holding back, you'll be in even bigger trouble."

Nikolai instructed the police officers to leave with Henry Gran. The old man went without a sound, and the wagon drove off down the road and into the misty haze. How much had Henry Gran told the Nazis? If they had some clues, it would only be a matter of time before they found the location of the painting.

Soli frowned. "What if someone else interrogates him, not you or your men?"

"No, I'll make sure we finish this case. I'll speak with him tomorrow morning and ask about the painting. Bringing it up here in the open was too risky."

"All right." She looked up at Nikolai. "I'd like to go now. Will you take me home?"

* * *

Nikolai stopped the car by the entrance to the art shop.

"There's someone on your lane. Stay here, Soli." Nikolai jumped out of the car and walked toward the man.

Soli's shoulders grew tense. Was the person here to force her to tell her secrets? As the man drew nearer and shook Nikolai's hand, Soli let out a relaxed breath. *Felix.* What a relief. She climbed out and ran over to hug the young man.

"I've figured out what the numbers you asked me about mean." Felix spoke low, checking to see if anyone could be listening.

"You have? Tell us." Soli dug her fingernails into her purse. She knew what they were looking for, but this could be the clue she needed to find the painting by Rubens. To think the art treasure could be within reach made her head spin.

They stepped closer together.

Felix held a hand next to his mouth and whispered, "The numbers are coordinates."

Soli slapped her forehead. "Of course. That makes sense."

Felix pulled a piece of paper out of his pocket. The fourteen numbers were lined up at the top, then his scribbles and unintelligible notes all the way down the page. He pointed to the last readable sentence at the bottom.

"Look here. Someone broke down the latitude and longitude by decimals. They used positive and negative numbers instead of the normal north, south, east, and west. It took me a while to understand the numbers and their correct position. You'll easily find your destination using this." He handed her the paper.

"So, the little ink blotches were periods and minus

signs?" Soli hugged Felix. "Thank you. I was going blind, staring at the figures, wondering what it meant."

"Well, the guy who wrote it meant to make it hard to understand. The long numeral looked like just that...a line-up of numbers."

"Splendid work, Felix." Nikolai's enthusiasm seemed to match Soli's.

"I took a quick look at the coordinates, and my guess is that the place you're looking for is on a road about an hour and a half's drive northwest from here. Although, I don't know what you expect to find," Felix said.

Nikolai put a hand on his back. "You're a valuable contributor to our work, and you've already suffered at the hands of someone who collaborates with the enemy. For now, it's safer for you to be kept in the dark regarding what we're trying to find. I promise, in due time, you'll discover what a great aid you've been to our cause."

"I'm continuing my work with the chiffer group. I just came from the office. Your friend George was there, helping Z with something."

Nikolai shook his hand again. "Thanks, Felix. We need your help, and my job is to keep you out of harm's way so you can continue working with us."

As the young man walked away, Soli grabbed Nikolai's arm. "We need to leave now. I'll just get a couple of things inside. And we should pick up Heddy first."

CHAPTER NINETEEN

DARKNESS HAD FALLEN upon Oslo hours earlier. Soli picked up a map and some other items from the office in the art shop. Thanks to Felix, she understood the numbers written in the ledger's margin. Leon Ruber had specified the position of the painting by using coordinates. He'd left out the signs for direction, minutes, and seconds to disguise the aligns and throw people off. It had confused her, but with Felix's help it now made sense.

She locked the door and hurried to the car where Nikolai was waiting. As she eased into the seat, she spotted a young man accompanying an elderly couple on the other side of the street. Soli's wristwatch said ten before nine. Ten minutes until curfew. Hopefully, they'd make it to their address in time and not break the deadline. She guessed the couple had hired the boy to take them safely home.

The murky evening absorbed any light on the street. Blackout-curtains covered every window, and most of the outdoor lamps were turned off or had covers. There were few places to pinpoint a direction, but some poles and roads had white marks to guide the way.

Driving was hazardous with the foggy weather they'd had all week. Nikolai barely dodged a bicyclist. The man's front light was shielded, and reflectors and panels were painted matt black. The only thing showing from behind was a white patch on the mudguard and a tiny dead lamp. The man lost his balance for a second but said nothing when he eyed a German patrol up the street. No one wanted trouble late at night, not even if they'd been offended and almost injured.

They picked up Heddy at the chiffer group and headed out of Oslo.

Because of war regulations, Nikolai's car had no inside lights, either. Soli handed Heddy the flashlight. "Can you hold this for me? I need to mark where we're headed." She unfolded the map in her lap, and with the use of a ruler and the directions from Felix, she imagined a grid and counted the latitude lines going northward. She located the right one and found the vertical longitude lines. With the correct meridian in place, Soli traced her finger until it met the chosen horizontal line. There she circled their destination on the map.

"I've got it," she said.

Now that they had the coordinates, there was not a moment to lose. They had to act fast and get a head start in case anyone else had discovered where to look for the painting by Peter Paul Rubens.

"I can't see clearly, but it seems like someone is following us out of town," Heddy said. "Those same lights have been on our tail for the last few streets."

Nikolai sped up. "Don't get how they could be. No one knows about this operation. Only the three of us."

"And Felix." Soli's eyes watered, and a sudden thickness filled her throat. "What if someone stopped him on his way home?"

"Oh, let it not be true." Heddy rubbed Soli's shoulder. "We must assume he made it home safely."

Nikolai hung a right on the next corner. "This is as fast as I can go without causing suspicion. We can't afford to be halted for speeding."

Soli frowned. "Henry Gran was friends with Leon Ruber. He could have heard where the Rubens painting is hidden, and the Nazis could have interrogated him. What if they know something and are headed in the same direction?"

Such terrifying thoughts. Rumors about paintings and stolen goods were always going around in the art community. Both art dealers and Nazi collectors had an interest in rare items.

"It is a possibility…isn't it, Nikolai?"

He gave Soli a quick glance and smiled. "Well, we'll have to get there before them, then."

Suddenly, he flung his arm out and pulled her down. "Duck," he yelled. "There's a German convoy up the road there. I should have gone another way. They might be checking papers for people going out of town tonight."

Soli held her head down. What would happen next?

"How are you doing in the back seat?" Nikolai asked.

Heddy touched his back. "I'm fine. We'll keep low until you tell us it's safe to get up."

Soli's patience wore thin. "What's happening, Nikolai?" she whispered.

"A soldier jumped out in front of our car. He's coming this way. Stay down. I'll go talk with him."

What seemed like ten minutes went by. The wait was

nerve racking, almost painful. They heard someone open the trunk, remove things, then slam the lid shut.

Soli rubbed her back. She crunched down lower. *Forget the pain. Ignore the terrifying fear.* She jerked when the door on the chauffeur's side opened. Nikolai climbed in and started driving again.

"Hold on, girls. Wait until we're out of sight." The car tootled along the road until Nikolai pushed the gas pedal to the speed limit. "We are in the clear...for now. The military truck drove back into town."

Soli sat up straight and stretched. They were in luck, not something they experienced often. She said a quick prayer, grateful to be on their way.

Heddy poked her head between them. "What happened back there? I was sure we'd have a German looking through our car windows. Whatever did you tell them?"

"Turns out those soldiers had a flat tire. They had a spare one in the back of the truck but no jack. I let them use mine and helped them out." Nikolai laughed. "Even if these men are mean, weapon-carrying brutes who show no mercy when they meet the enemy, you'll sometimes find young men like those two, who don't know how to change a tire or iron a shirt."

"There are headlights behind us again," Heddy said.

Nikolai stepped on the gas pedal, and the vehicle roared down the road.

Soli's stomach knotted. "But if they don't have the ledger or the coordinates, how would they know where to look? The Jewish family who owned the painting is gone. Jacob, too." Her hands tightened into fists. "Then how?"

Nikolai rubbed his eyes. "It could be others, unfaithful

servants or friends of the family who don't want trouble with the Gestapo. Or someone tormented into telling secrets. Even an associate could have knowledge about their art."

"The German police have ways of getting that information," Heddy said.

"Unfortunately." Nikolai remained calm but determined. "It could be someone driving in the same direction as us, but we're not going to take that chance." He checked the rearview mirror. "They're gaining on us. I'm going as fast as I can without losing control and running us off the road."

Shocked and horrified they could lose the fight Soli squeezed the ruler until her fingers grew sore. She turned her head again to see if the car was still following. No headlights beamed behind them. Was the car just beyond the bend? She let go of the ruler, and with trembling hands she placed the things on the floor by her feet. They were doing the right thing and were not about to give up now. They had to find the Rubens rendition and get it to safety.

Nikolai had grabbed the steering wheel at ten and two o'clock and stared into the light from the headlights up ahead. He kept glancing into the rearview mirror. "Do you see them?"

"No, they must be farther back. It's hard to tell when the route keeps winding like a snake through this hilly region."

"Let me keep an eye on what's going on behind us," Heddy said. "You two watch the road up ahead. Soli can be on the lookout for any moose or deer. They're more likely to wander into the road after dark."

"Hold tight," Nikolai said, baring his teeth. He

suddenly swerved to the left, throwing Soli toward the door.

"What are you doing?" Heddy cried out.

The tires screeched as they rounded the corner, barely dodging a large rock on the side of the road. The rutted dirt lane had tall grass in the middle and was filled with potholes and rocky gravel. Nikolai veered away from some of the largest depressions. Holding on to the door with her right hand and the edge of her seat with the left, Soli bobbed from one side to the other. Then the road widened a bit, and Nikolai parked the car by a fence and switched off the motor and lights.

They sat in silence for a minute, a chance to breathe before they continued the search. Now what?

"Soli, can you get out the map?" Nikolai stretched for the flashlight that had fallen on the floor next to his seat.

She handed him the map. "Here, let me hold the light for you."

He searched the map and pointed to the circle she'd drawn earlier. "Is this according to the coordinates you had?"

"Yes, and it looks like an out-of-the-way place. There's a road that goes there, but I doubt if there are many cabins or farms."

"Maybe Leon Ruber hid the painting in a cave, on an isolated farmstead, or something...I don't know," Heddy said.

Nikolai stretched to reach the glove compartment and pulled out a compass. "This should help us find the way on the map."

Soli turned her head to check if they were alone. Darkness had swallowed up the path out toward the main road. Not a single beam of moonlight cut through the heavy clouds. Nothing lit up the obscure landscape. The evening could not have been blacker and murkier. She jumped in her seat as an owl hooted in the forest surrounding them.

Nikolai touched her arm. "We're all right. Even if they were following, they were probably too far back to see us turn down this dirt road."

Heddy leaned forward. "We just have to find the place before they do."

"We will." Nikolai quickly found their position on the map. "We need to go that direction," he said, pointing northward.

They got out of the car, and Nikolai aimed the flashlight in the direction he'd indicated. He folded up the map and placed it into his pocket.

"If we walk through the woods, we'll reach our journey's end in about twenty minutes. The road winds down near a river and follows it to a lake up ahead. It's a much longer route, and even by car, it will take them close to an hour to get there. Are you ready, Soli?"

She nodded. Her mind spun with frightening scenes of not making it in time, getting caught, and Nazis disappearing with the artwork, their evil laughter echoing through the thickets in the dead of night. Still, they had Nikolai there. He would protect them. She took hold of Heddy's outstretched hand.

Nikolai smiled and started walking. "Now, let's go find your painting."

~ CAPITOLO V ~
ANTWERP, 1613

THE MOON WAS high, and a shadow crept across the windowsill in the parlor of Isaac Ruber's residence in Antwerp. Everyone had retired for the night. The servants were in their quarters. All was quiet. Only the soothing sound of wood crackling in the fireplace broke the silence. A candle flickered on a hutch against the left wall, and above it hung Fabiola's new painting. The rich, bold colors and elaborate gilded frame stood well against the white wall with dark wooden trim.

On her second visit to the master painter's studio, Fabiola had learned he favored historical symbolism and certain images of a good life. He'd shown her a portrait he'd painted of himself sitting lovingly with his wife, Isabella. The couple sat in front of a honeysuckle branch.

"Do you know what it means?" he'd asked. "What does that particular flower symbolize?"

She'd had to admit her shortcomings when it came to the symbolism of flowers and nature. But Master Rubens had patiently explained.

"The honeysuckle is a symbol of love, gentility, loyalty, and devotion. I wanted that in the portrait of Isabella and myself. Would you like me to paint the honeysuckle in the background of yours?"

She'd happily agreed to his suggestion. Ciphers of devotion and fidelity should ever be welcome in her home.

Isabella had come by the studio that day, her hair swept up and fastened with lace and pearls, and bracelets with colorful jewels on her wrists.

"I hope he is kind to you," she'd said in a pleasant voice. "He can be rather strict when immersed in his paintings." Isabella's small, heart-shaped mouth tilted upward, giving the impression of sweetness, but also humor. A little girl about Annarosa's age had stood behind her mother's skirts.

"This is Clara. She's named after many Claras in our family." Isabella had stroked her stomach. "And we're hoping this will be a boy."

While Master Rubens had outlined the painting, the two women had spoken about running a household, as well as their thoughts about flowers, clothing, and motherhood.

"I should like you to call on me again," Isabella had said when Fabiola was bracing to leave. "I am certain we can become good friends."

Fabiola now held her first confidant in Antwerp, a close friend she could spend time with.

She pulled up a chair and sat to admire her padre's latest acquisition. He'd granted her birthday wish, Master Rubens had received his wage, and all was well. On the back corner of the painting was the message written in Master Rubens's own hand. She could not be more pleased.

Even her daughter had clapped her little hands as the footman hung the painting on the wall, thrilled to see the reflection of her Mama, Rosa...as she called herself...and the two dogs. Fabiola had then followed her to the nursery, kissed her goodnight, and told her a story about a princess who had her portrait painted by an ogre who changed and turned out to be the kindest, gentlest man. Annarosa had let out a burst of giggles when they came to the part where the two dogs had to sit still for the artist.

Fabiola climbed the stairs and slowly wandered the hallway to her room. She would undress herself. Nava had fallen asleep hours ago, and Fabiola did not want to wake her.

Eli had been away for several weeks on a trade mission to the Indies. She prayed the vessel would bring him safely home. Her husband was always polite and friendly, although not present in her life. Not that she expected that of him. Their nuptial had been arranged by their fathers, but she still hoped their marriage would be more than a union of convenience. Oh, that they would fall deeply in love and be everything to and for each other. Maybe those were the silly notions of a young woman, but she sincerely wanted their time together to be more than polite conversation.

She sat down by her writing desk and pulled a quill pen, an ink bottle, and a piece of paper out of the drawer. She'd thought about this for a long time. It was time to close a chapter of her life and live in the present. The artist known as Michelangelo Merisi da Caravaggio was dead. The man she knew would be part of her. "Pray, give me a moment," she whispered. "Some secrets refuse to stay silent. I will write what my heart tells me to. It will be spirited and move me toward a satisfying future."

Salutations, Messer Michelangelo.

My compliments on your life, contributions, and praise.

    This evening I write, knowing this letter will never reach you. It pains me that I had to leave and could not step in when you were in need of a friend. What we had was precious to me, but I had no choice.

    I have been wed these last four years, and my husband and I have a sweet daughter, Annarosa.

    Messere, I must tell you how I have received closure. Do you remember Signor Peter Paul Rubens? As a young man he resided in Italy, and while in Rome he became acquainted with the sublime work of Caravaggio. In search of an artist who could paint a portrait of Annarosa and myself, I chose him because of his admiration for your art. The result is admirable, and I believe you would approve.

    Now, I must step forward. With the help of God, I must prevail and be pleased with the good fortune I have been allotted in life.

I ask for God's blessing upon you.
    With hope, Fabiola Ruber

She folded the message, melted some wax, and dripped the edges to seal the paper. With great care, she pressed the stamp with the letters FR into the soft wax and watched it dry. She placed the letter in the back of the bottom drawer underneath her jewelry box. Then, pushing the drawer back into place, Fabiola smiled. Her heart was finally healing, and she was ready to embrace life with her husband in Antwerp. When Eli returned from his travels tomorrow, she would take the time to truly know him and find his heart. She would show her husband the portrait and explain the reason why Rubens had added the honeysuckle.

CHAPTER TWENTY

AS THE TRAIL opened to a clearing, a turf-roofed log house came into view. Small rung windows painted blue gave the cottage a cheerful expression, despite the dark blinds preventing any light from escaping.

The fog had lifted, and they crossed a lawn around the side to the front entrance. High on the hillside, the view over the valley below was breathtaking. The moon shone behind a wispy cloud, giving a feeble glow to a path winding down to the end of a dirt road. But the ominous weather was about to return. As Soli stood there, the mirror of light on the surface of the lake beyond the road was receding. Before long, the view would once again be nothing but a murky wall of fog.

A smaller cottage on the grassy hill matched the main house. Other than that, Soli had not seen any other buildings for miles around. According to the coordinates, this was the place.

"We don't know who's behind that door," Soli whispered.

"Whoever it is, we're about to meet them." Nikolai stepped up the stone stairs and knocked.

Soli and Heddy followed, their eyes meeting, apprehensive but curious. What would they find? Would their mission be fruitful or end in a dreadful disaster? Soli straightened her back. Any time now, that door would open.

A man's brusque voice thundered through the solid wood. "Who's there? We carry guns, and we're not afraid to use them."

Nikolai nudged Soli. "You should speak. As a woman, you'll be less threatening."

She swallowed hard and leaned closer to the door. "My name is Soli Hansen, and I'm here on behalf of the Ruber family. I believe you're in possession of something that belongs to them, an item they've asked you to take care of."

"Are you alone?" He must have seen the three of them from behind the curtains, but it was best to act politely to get a foot inside.

"I'm in the company of my friends, Heddy and Detective Nikolai Lange. Please open so I can explain."

The sound of four different locks cut through the soft mist. The door screeched on its hinges as a middle-aged, bearded man opened. He had a pistol in his hand. Behind him stood another fellow wearing the same stern expression and appearing to be about the same age. The second man's face was clean-shaven, revealing saggy cheeks and bushy eyebrows. His shotgun pointed straight at Soli.

Nikolai discreetly supported Soli's elbow. He understood. Facing weapons held by two men who did not seem afraid to shoot someone who had trespassed on their property caused her hands to shake. She cleared her throat and lifted her chin. *No time for fear, Soli. Just say what you came for.*

"May we come in?" She rubbed her arms. "It's a little chilly, and we want to explain why we're here."

The two men, still scowling, kept up their guard-like positions.

Nikolai took a step forward. "Can we put the weapons away? We all need to trust each other. We understand your hesitation. I mean, here we are, three strangers on your doorstep, late in the evening and with no warning or notice about our arrival. But we are on a mission, one that has become a charge of life and death, and we are equally worried about who you are." He stretched his neck a little. "But from what I see, you display a Norwegian flag above the mirror in your hallway. I would say we're on the same side in this war, and from our investigation, this is the place to find the answers we're seeking."

The bearded man lowered his hand and stuck the pistol into his pocket. "Very well. You may all enter. Not knowing who you were, we had to take precautions."

He pushed the door all the way open and let them come into the hallway. Clippings of King Haakon VII, Queen Maud, and Crown Prince Olav V accompanied the flag on the wall. This was a patriotic home. Soli slipped out of her shoes and was about to hang up her coat upon a hook.

He waved her into the living room. "You'd better leave your shoes and jackets on. If you're here on a vital, covert operation, others may follow. You never know how quickly you might need to run back out that door.

Soli put her shoes back on and proceeded into the living area. The men invited them to take a seat around the dining room table. Out of habit, Soli turned to see what hung on the walls. A spruce cabinet painted with flowing lines and colorful floral design sat in the corner. Framed black-and-white drawings of rugged trolls adorned the walls on either side. Soli did not have to check the signature of the artist. Only Theodor Kittelsen made renditions like that. He was famous for his illustrations of creatures from folklore and fairytales. She suppressed the desire to discuss how they'd purchased the graphics and refocused her thoughts on the major reason for their visit. Like the man had said, someone might find their way there and show up at any time.

"I'm Per," the bearded man said. "This is my brother Paul. Now, you mentioned the Ruber family." He peered at his brother, who gave him an affirmative nod. "Leon Ruber rented the smaller cottage here one summer. He brought his family up, and we became close friends."

Paul cut in. "We had much in common, even if they were a Jewish family. Not long after that, he showed up one day and asked if we would take care of some things for him. He said he'd return for the items once it was safe again."

Per nodded. "We'd heard rumors of war and trouble for those of the Jewish faith. It must have been about..." He looked at his brother. "About five years ago?"

Soli leaned forward. "What objects did he ask you to safekeep?"

"We have here an old set of china, a box of jewelry, and one painting."

Soli's fingers tingled. She had difficulty sitting still and would prefer to skip all other explanations.

But Per continued. "At the time, we didn't understand. Why would the family not be safe, and why hide their valuables?"

"We're sorry to inform you that Leon Ruber and his family have been arrested." Nikolai paused then said, "Deported."

Paul stood and started pacing the floor in circles. "We own a wireless and receive some broadcasts up here." He stopped abruptly and looked at Nikolai.

Nikolai put his hands up. "I'm not here to bother anyone about having a radio. In fact, I think it's great if you have one and can listen to our broadcasts from London."

Paul relaxed his shoulders. "We heard news about Jews being taken from their homes and sent away. But tell me…are they dead?"

"We don't know, but so far, Jews who are deported have not returned," Heddy said.

Per put his elbows on the table and leaned his head in his cupped hands. "We just didn't think it would happen this way, that our Jewish friends would be arrested, and someone else would come for the painting. How did you know where to find us?"

"The owner left us several clues," Soli said.

"Clues? Well, you must tell us about those some other time." Per stood and joined his brother in the center of the room. "Should we?"

The other fellow nodded and gestured for them to follow them into the living room.

A red velvet sofa sat against the wall, and above it hung the painting.

Soli gawked. It was like seeing a view for the first time, like having the fog lift and the light come in. Her smile widened as Heddy squeezed her arm from behind. Soli stood in awe. How could someone paint anything so beautiful?

Nikolai put his arm around both girls. "You did it, Soli. You found the Rubens."

"With your help, mind you."

She went closer, taking in all the details. Fabiola and the little girl had matching dresses. The dogs were the same as in the other painting she'd seen. The material in the background, the detail to the clothes, and every facial feature—everything was perfect.

"We've wondered why her hair isn't styled like in most of the artwork from that time period," Paul said.

"I believe she chose to wear it that way."

Per leaned forward, supporting his hands on the back of a chair. "You look as if you recognize the woman in the painting."

"I do. Her name is Fabiola. She's depicted in another one by a different artist. The little girl must be her daughter. She looks so much like her mother."

Heddy pointed to Fabiola's neckline. "She's also wearing the same piece of jewelry with the star of David."

Per sighed. "How can that be? From what we've been told, this is an unknown rendition by Rubens, one kept in the Ruber family since it was painted in the early seventeenth century."

"I'm afraid we don't have time to explain. Perhaps another day. For now, we ask you to trust us. There are others looking for this. Nazi art hunters. They could show up here at any minute, and we need to move the painting somewhere safe." Heddy kept checking the window in the dining room.

"We thought it was safe here," Paul said.

Nikolai shook his head. "It was. But not anymore."

Per stretched his hands above the sofa and removed the frame from the nail on the wall. "We've had the woman and child on our wall for a long time. We'll miss them."

His brother agreed. "Hopefully, sometime in the future, we could get together, and you can enlighten us more about the artist and the people he painted."

"I'd like that," Soli said.

"There's something else that might interest you." Paul turned the painting backward on the sofa and pointed to an inscription in small letters in the upper left corner of the canvas. "Brother, go get something to help her see better."

Per opened a drawer in the side table next to the sofa, pulled out a flashlight and a magnifying glass, and gave them to Soli. "We hope you can explain the meaning."

She went close and traced her finger along the coarse canvas. The lettering was tiny and wound in twists and turns, as if the artist himself had written them.

In ricordo del grande Caravaggio.
Che il tuo talento risplenda sempre, anche attraverso gli
altri.
Tua, Fabiola

Soli read the words. "In memory of the great Caravaggio. May your talent always shine, also through others. Yours, Fabiola."

Soli sighed. Another affirmation that she'd loved him.

Per protested. "Caravaggio? But Rubens painted this, didn't he?"

"Does it make sense to you?" Paul asked.

Soli smiled. "Yes, it does. We know Fabiola had a special bond to Caravaggio. I believe that's why she chose to have this portrait done by an artist who followed in his footsteps and used the chiaroscuro technique."

Per squinted. "What does that mean?"

"The artist illuminates light from the dark," Soli said.

Both brothers widened their eyes.

"Yes, I can see that now," Paul said. "How interesting. We've always thought the contrast was sublime and effective to bring out the two models."

"And you can tell the woman is the focus of attention in this picture and not the dogs. Not even the daughter is accentuated as much as Fabiola is," Soli said. She pointed to the empty spot above the sofa. "Look, your wallpaper is faded except where the picture has hung. Do you have something else to hang up there in case anyone else comes here? It shouldn't look like a framed piece is missing."

Per put a finger up in the air. "Good thing my brother and I are hobby artists. Can you get the watercolor under the bed, Paul? The one you did last year?"

Paul frowned. "But it's not worthy of the prime spot in the living room."

"Never mind. Just do it."

"All right." Paul shuffled away and then returned from the bedroom with a framed watercolor about the same size as the Rubens. He hung it on the nail and took a step back. "How embarrassing. I hid it under the bed and never intended for anyone to see it."

Per pulled the tablecloth off the dining room table and handed it to Nikolai. "Here. It's clean, and you can use it to wrap the painting."

Soli jumped as a bell in the ceiling rang.

"Oh, no," Per said.

Nikolai hurried to the window and looked out. "What's the alarm for?"

Per huffed. "Visitors...or more likely, enemies. We have a wire attached to the sheep grid that crosses the road down below. It goes through the bushes and up to our house to warn us of any cars coming this way." He patted Soli's shoulder. "We look forward to hearing the entire story, but there's no time right now."

Nikolai asked, "How long until they get here?"

"The lane winds and turns until they meet a dead end by the lake." Per narrowed his eyes. "About eight or ten minutes, maybe. They'll park their car next to ours then find the path up the hill. The walk takes five minutes. Seven, at the most."

Nikolai took Soli aside. "I know you don't want to tear yourself away from the artwork, but it's time, Soli." He spoke low. "We need to get the painting out of here now. After we make a run through the woods and back to the car, I'll drop you and Heddy off on the outskirts of Oslo then drive through the night and hand the piece over to Thor Hammer. He'll make sure it's safe until we need to move it somewhere else."

"I hate to see it go already and wish I had just a few more minutes." She shook her head vigorously. "No, it's back to reality. I know you'll take it to safety."

He stroked her cheek. "Your enthusiasm brings all of us into your enchanted world of art. We could listen to you forever, but those men out there will be here at any moment."

Heddy joined them. "Let's hope there are no road-blocks or German convoys going your way. Take the back roads, and you should be fine."

Nikolai wrapped the tablecloth around the painting.

"When will you be back?" Soli asked.

"Two hours' drive up there, deliver the painting in the dark of night, then two hours back to Oslo."

Heddy turned to the brothers. "The so-called visitors are probably after the painting. We suspect the Nazis want it for their own treasure coffers."

Per stood, legs apart, and folded his arms across his chest. "This is our home. We will not flee. Besides, as we said earlier, we are not afraid to protect ourselves. We're far off the beaten track up here; no one will know if a Nazi or two disappears."

Soli's widened eyes met Heddy's. Those old teddy bears were much more dangerous than they looked. What had they been through in life to toughen them that way?

Paul scurried across the floor and peeked out behind the curtain. "Flickering lights down below. The car is approaching. They'll soon park and start on the path up here."

"Did you come up the trail through the woods?" Per asked.

Heddy nodded.

He flipped his hand toward a door on the opposite side of the living room. "Quick, go out the door in the bedroom. It'll take you back the way you came."

Nikolai secured the painting and pushed the girls ahead to the bedroom. As Soli took a step to the side to let Heddy pass, her foot fell through a broken floor plank. She cried out in pain, sat down, and with her hands slowly lifted her leg out of the hole.

"Oh, my goodness. I should have had that fixed ages ago. I curse myself for putting it off," Per said.

Nikolai stretched his hand out and pulled Soli up. "Can you walk?"

Treading carefully did not even work. "I can't run anywhere like this. So sorry. You two will have to leave without me."

Heddy steadied Soli's arm. "I'm not leaving you. Nikolai, you need to get the painting to safety. Soli and I will hide somewhere."

"We have a small storage basement, and we can bring the young ladies back to town later," Per said.

Heddy let out a long breath. "That'll have to do. Now, run, Nikolai. We'll see you tomorrow." She turned and went into the kitchen with the brothers.

Once again, things were out of hand. Once again, they had to come up with a different plan, one they had not prepared and not expected.

Soli turned to Nikolai. His eyes looked like those of a distressed puppy.

"We'll be fine, Nikolai."

"Your faith in this rescue operation is resilient, Soli. You don't doubt for a second we can avoid the enemy getting their hands on this painting."

"I have to believe we'll succeed when we do good things." She stretched up and kissed his lips.

He returned her affection then opened his eyes. "I didn't dare hope you felt this way."

Despite her throbbing foot and the enemy at the door, she gave him a heartfelt smile. "Now you know." She pushed him toward the exit. "Run. And be careful. Remember that more important than rescuing the Rubens rendition is to get yourself to safety."

He tucked the painting snug under his arm and disappeared into the darkness outside.

CHAPTER TWENTY-ONE

SOLI HOBBLED INTO the kitchen, as Per pushed a cat off a woven rug in the middle of the wooden floor. He kicked the runner to the side and opened a trapdoor underneath. A narrow ladder descended into a dark room below.

Heddy went first.

"There's a light switch on your left," Paul said. "No one can see the light from the outside."

Heddy flipped the switch and lifted her hands to help Soli down. The brothers closed the hatchet and replaced the rug just as someone banged on the door.

They could hear the voices upstairs, which meant they could be heard, also. Heddy found a stool and pointed for Soli to sit, while Heddy took a seat on the bottom step.

The brothers waited before answering the door, no doubt stalling to give Nikolai a good head start on his way through the woods.

The knock came a second and third time before they opened.

"Good evening, I must be lost," a man said. "I've

looked everywhere for an address in this almost unap-
proachable place in the boondocks."

Suddenly, Heddy gawked and covered her mouth with
her fingers.

Soli lifted her eyebrows and put her hands up. What
had her friend so disturbed?

Heddy removed her hand and with a concerned look
mouthed, "My father."

The brothers must have decided on a less fiendish
approach without guns or threats. Per's voice rang loud
and clear. "It's a long way back to town, but you get there
by going the same road you came. Drive safely."

It sounded as if Per tried to shut the door but was
stopped.

"Not so fast," Vengen called out. "May I come in and
ask you a couple of questions first?"

"Enter. Would you like a cup of coffee?"

"Certainly, and you probably have something stronger
to add to it."

The sound of footsteps crossed the floor, and chairs
were pulled out. They sat in the dining room. Would
Heddy's father grab the drawings by Kittelsen off the wall
while he was there? Someone in Vengen's position knew
no boundaries.

"I have it from a reliable source that a Jewish family
used to visit this area."

Per said, "Jewish? We're not Jewish. Besides, we keep
to ourselves and don't have many visitors anymore."

It sounded like a flat palm slammed on the table, and
Vengen yelled. "Stop this nonsense. They came to this
area, and I believe they left something of value. That item
now belongs to the Reich."

Soli's frightened eyes met Heddy's. What were they to

do? The two brothers would certainly defend themselves and their home if they met an enemy. In this case, Heddy's father was a threat and had entered their house in an attempt to steal the Rubens.

"Tell us what you're after, and maybe we can help you," Per suggested.

Was that a smart move? Why invite Heddy's father deeper into the discussion about the painting and risk revealing something about it?

"You stupid man," Vengen said. He was getting hoarse from raising his voice. "The old book, of course. I want Ruber's family ledger. I've heard it's a well of information about their treasures."

Relieved, Soli looked at Heddy and smiled. Heddy's father was not after the painting. At least, not yet. The ledger, on the other hand, was in danger, but for the time being only Soli knew where it was.

The drama upstairs was still not over.

"I'm not afraid to use it," Vengen shouted. Apparently, he had pulled his gun on the brothers.

Per said, "Why would you do that? You'll not get any answers if you shoot us."

"I'll wound one of you first."

Heddy came very close and whispered in Soli's ear. "I don't know if my father is capable of killing anyone."

Soli whispered back. "Let's hope he's just bluffing."

The tension became more heated.

"The Ruber family came here," Vengen yelled. "You must know something."

Per kept his calm. "We've had many people stay in the cabin over the years. It doesn't mean we have information about their personal lives."

The bottom step creaked as Heddy changed her position.

"What was that?" Vengen said, suspicion in his angry voice.

"No worries. This is an old house," Paul said. "The wind often sweeps around the corner, tricking us into believing in ghouls and other creatures."

Something bounced across the floor above the girls' heads and jumped into the dining room. It had to be the cat they saw sleeping earlier.

"Ah, there's the culprit," Per said, unruffled. "Now, where were we? Yes, you asked about an old book. Ledger, ledger… Brother, could he be thinking about *that* ledger?"

"Maybe," Paul answered. "I'll go get it."

Footsteps moved into the kitchen. Then the sound of opening and closing cabinets doors and drawers and strides back to the dining table.

"Here's the ledger we've kept for years. It has a list of all the visitors in our cabin down below. You'll find the name of Leon Ruber there, also."

Soli strained to hear. Someone flipped through pages, then there was a loud bang as if Vengen threw the book down.

"Imbecile. I'll stay until you give me the information I want. One way or another, you will tell me what I need to know and hand over the old ledger, not this…this roster."

What happened next, Soli could only guess based on the sounds emanating from above. Chairs flung aside, cups broke on the floor, scuffling between three older men. When the chaos ceased, it certainly sounded like the two brothers had outmanned Heddy's father.

Per's voice was coarser now. "We've had enough of your

babble, coming here late at night, asking us to deliver things we know nothing about, and frightening our poor cat. I suggest you get up off the floor and disappear for good. This is our home, our property. We can easily rid ourselves of you, hide your body, and dump your car in the lake. It will cost us nothing, and no one will know where to find you."

Heddy's eyes widened. She leaned close to Soli and whispered, "No matter what, I don't want the brothers to kill my father. I should go up there and tell them—"

She stood, but Soli pulled her back down and shook her head.

Vengen attempted one last try. "Now, you listen—"

The house was quiet. A minute went by. Two minutes. Soli held on to her thigh, trying to keep Heddy from noticing her shaking limbs. The unbearable feeling of disappearing into time— not knowing what would happen, worrying, and waiting—looped around in Soli's mind.

Heddy stretched to listen. She shook her head and slumped, burying her face in her hands, sobbing soundlessly. Soli bent forward and took hold of her.

The delay seemed endless. Not that they had an allotted time to wait for the outcome of a shootout. There was no way of knowing how it would end, and it tore at Soli like ripping open a seam. What if it had been Far up there, giving his life's performance?

Heddy lifted her head and met Soli's eyes. She mouthed, "What is happening to my father?"

A person moved across the floor. The worn wooden planks creaked with each step.

Soli held her breath.

Then Vengen spoke, sounding conquered and tired. "Well, it's obvious I've been misinformed. According to my source who knew Isaac Ruber, the ledger was supposed to be here. This is a dead end in more ways than one. I'll find that old book. Someone has it."

The door slammed, and Soli's shoulders drooped. Thank goodness, he had left.

ONE WEEK LATER
SATURDAY, 14 OCTOBER 1944

THE SQUARE NEAR the department store was still crowded. Men were trading goods, and women were lined up to buy salted herring or fresh cod. Heddy was on her way to meet Nikolai and Soli at the art shop when she heard someone call her name.

"Hedvig!"

She looked up and into her father's stern face. A rush of frustration shot through her body. Just the sight of him caused her to clench her fists—well-fed and wearing his fashionable pin-striped suit. Women probably thought him distinguished. All Heddy could think about was his outrageous behavior when he came looking for the ledger the other night.

He pushed the glasses up on his nose and placed his hands on his back.

"Well, there you are."

"Yes, here I am." A ridiculous thing to answer. But the truth was, she did not know what to say to him. Heddy was certain he'd not mention his endeavor to find the ledger or his collaboration with Heinz Walter, but she could say something about Bech. She'd not seen his two-timing junior around town lately.

"Where's your assistant," she asked. "Doesn't he work with you?"

He pulled a crooked grin. "So, you are interested, after all?"

"No, definitely not. I'm just making conversation, Father."

He frowned. "Hmm. Well, I've sent him back to Germany on the same plane as my commanding officer. Sophus Bech is a wimp when it comes to serious matters. He's a lad with a big mouth and an even bigger ego. I can tell he has potential, though. By the time he returns, I hope to get a fiercer, more unbendable assistant." He handed her a letter. "He asked me to give you this."

Heddy huffed. A personal letter from Bech. Her name was on the envelope. She stuffed it into her pocket and was about to ask her father if he'd met her sisters when he cut her off.

"I'm on my way to Amundsen's for dinner. Come join me."

Heddy couldn't bear the thought of joining him. Not another meal at that place and not with her father. She had no problem pulling a white lie.

"No, thank you, Father. I've an errand to run for my boss."

She stretched her hand high in the air and waved. "Ah, there he is. He's extremely strict, and I'm afraid I need to hurry. So sorry. Enjoy your dinner, Father."

Heddy ran down the street and mingled with a crowd of people on the other side of the square. She did not turn around. Her Father most likely stood baffled, wondering who she worked for. She snuck behind a group of women in line at a potato stand. Of course, no one was there to meet her, but it made a good excuse to get away without further explanation.

* * *

Soli was closing the shop when Nikolai and Heddy showed up.

"I have cake," Nikolai said, and gave Soli a kiss. He placed a paper box on the table.

"Oh, what kind?" Soli asked.

"Does it matter? It's cake." Heddy peeked inside the carton. "Mmm, chocolate. I hope it has lots of chocolate and fewer potatoes."

Nikolai smiled. "Well, let's find out. My cousin made it. She works in a bakery."

Soli got plates and forks and cut them each a slice. "I'm sure it's tasty."

Heddy took a big bite. "Oh, this is good. She even added some pudding between the layers." She had another chew. "Nikolai, this is the best sweet treat I've had in a very long time." She leaned back in the chair. "I have some exciting news. I ran into my father, and he knows nothing about my involvement with the ledger or the painting."

She gave Soli a concerned look. "He also mentioned a senior officer who'd returned to Germany."

"Heinz Walter?"

"He didn't mention names, but I am certain that's who he meant. It feels safer, knowing that brute is farther away from us."

"For now."

Heddy pulled the envelope out of her pocket. "But my father gave me this." She opened the letter and read:

Dear Miss Vengen,

When you read this, I will be stationed in Germany. The Reich is pleased with my performance, and I have been offered a post there for the next months.

I have a confession. I bumped into your friend a while back. I saw you together on a bench by the church one day and became enraged with jealousy. Why can someone else spend time with you? Why not me? To find out more about her and what you have in common, I stole her purse. It was an ugly purse, and I threw it away. Please give her my apologies.

Until we meet again,
  Sophus Bech.

Soli burst out laughing. "He's right about the purse. It was ugly. And this is proof that he assaulted me."

"No, no. According to Bech, he didn't assault you… He bumped into you," Nikolai said, winking at her.

Heddy helped herself to another piece of cake. "Haha, the man's intolerable. My father said Bech's transfer to Germany was not because of his assistant's excellence but rather to toughen up a boastful coward."

"Let's hope he doesn't return a monster after his training. He seems like an impressionable man, one who follows blindly even though his heart is somewhere else." Soli poured water into three glasses. "Nikolai, what happened to Henry Gran? Did he ever mention the painting?"

"No, he didn't say anything about that. The old man is

doing time for abducting Felix. He worked both sides and staged his own disappearance."

"But he was very uncomfortable when he gave the art lecture at the Winthers' residence," Soli said.

"True. His performance there was not voluntary. Still, we have no idea which side he'll choose once he's served his sentence. We need to make sure Z and Felix are safe, also."

Heddy put a hand on her stomach. "I'm stuffed. Nikolai, tell us more about your trip with the Rubens painting. How's our friend Thor Hammer these days?"

"Thor gives everything to the resistance group in the Kongsberg area. Living dangerously, he's the complete representative of bravery, dedication, and love for his country. Those *boys in the woods* are down-to-earth men who stop at nothing in their fight against our invaders."

Soli put down her fork. "This isn't the first painting he's taken care of for us. Did you discuss how to protect it?"

Nikolai's deep-blue eyes crinkled at the edges. "He said you'd already given him a lecture on art preservation."

It was never long between smiles or friendly glances from her handsome detective. He helped himself to more cake. "They'll keep the painting in the mountain cabin, but it may be necessary to transport it and other items to a better place when winter sets in."

"I'd like to be informed when that happens," Soli said eagerly. "We should help them move the artwork."

Nikolai's face turned somber as his brows drew together. "It's a dangerous mission, Soli."

Heddy leaned back. "Do you think you can stop her when it comes to protecting her precious art?"

"No. It would be useless to even try." He took hold of Soli's hand and gently squeezed it.

"We wouldn't have been able to solve our cases of missing and stolen art pieces if it hadn't been for your help, Soli," Heddy said.

"But you're the ones who—"

Nikolai shook his head. "No, Heddy's right. This resistance group needs you."

"Thank you both." Soli got up and paced the room. "Now, for my bit of news."

Sporadic thoughts danced in her mind. A combination of excitement and nervous anticipation. She'd kept this thought to herself since the last time she'd studied the old ledger at her father's home. The notion had churned and worked itself into a powerful plea—one she was ready to share with her two best friends. She stopped and faced Heddy and Nikolai, and their eyes focused on her.

"There's one more." She took a deep breath. "It won't be easy, and we'll no doubt walk into danger and trouble." She paused then blurted out. "Leon Ruber hid another painting. I found the entry in the ledger and already know who painted it." She twisted her hands and smiled with anticipation. "I need your help to find it."

"I knew it," Heddy said. "You've been acting secretive." She rose from her chair and hugged Soli. "Come peril and life-threatening situations. The boys and I will be there with you every step. Just let me know when you're ready to get started." She picked up her jacket and placed the beret on her head. "I have to run. Thank you again, Nikolai. The cake was wonderful."

She hurried out the door. Every day was a risk in Heddy's life, but she never gave up fighting for their country.

Nikolai stood and swept Soli up in his arms. "You can count me in, too." He leaned in and let his forehead rest against hers. For a moment, floating through time and space, they were as one.

His kiss was a promise of goodness and truth. She looked into his deep-blue eyes. Wonder and curiosity swirled in her mind. She knew the next mission would be severe, but she would not find better people to share that journey with.

AUTHOR'S NOTE

In this novel, I've mentioned several real-life people. One is the pro-Nazi Minister President Vidkun Quisling, who headed the Norwegian state administration from 1942-1945. Quisling was also a dealer and collector of fine art. He was executed after the war for high treason.

Of course, Adolf Hitler is another. In his autobiography *Mein Kampf*, Hitler describes how he initially wanted to become an artist. His great admiration for and interest in art continued throughout his life. The art project by German Nazi soldiers stationed in Norway was the real deal, too. They were part of a special art squadron. At all times during the war, a group of 45 artists served in various countries, making art an important part of the lives of the occupying forces.

Another who is briefly mentioned is the Norwegian Crown Prince during WWII. Olav V wanted to stay behind with the Norwegian people during the occupation, but he had to follow the king and the government into exile. He received war decoration from several countries for his contribution against the Hitler regime.

The painters mentioned were part of the renaissance and baroque art movements in Europe. Caravaggio developed the well-known chiaroscuro technique, and many other artists followed in his footsteps.

For me, it was a joy to describe the master painter Peter Paul Rubens of Antwerp and his wife Isabella. I was mesmerized by a painting he did in 1609 called *The Honeysuckle Bower*. This work is full of symbolism. The honeysuckle itself is a symbol of love, gentility, devotion, and even a protection from evil.

The Honeysuckle Bower also shows Peter and Isabella Rubens as a beautiful couple, holding hands, portraying their union. There are cultural aspects shown in Isabella's traditional hat and his gentlemanlike attitude. She is feminine, delicately holding her fan, while Rubens shows how he is willing to protect her by keeping his hand on the hilt of his sword. The pumpkin-colored hose gives the master painter a whimsical look and matches her wine-red skirt. I adore this piece of art because it shows not only his amazing artistic talent but the love he shared with Isabella. The couple had seventeen more years together before Isabella died of the Bubonic Plague, when she was just 34 years old. Rubens remarried and lived another eleven years before he died in Antwerp in 1640.

There's another baroque painting of a two-year-old girl that I used as inspiration for the story. There's a discussion if this is actually by Rubens, but I used this painting to describe the way Annarosa looks when she goes to have her portrait done. If you search the internet for the name Anna Ludovica aged two, you will find this picture.

Another man who is briefly mentioned is Ragnvald

Alfred Roscher Lund. He was a Norwegian military officer who saw what was coming years before WWII broke loose. He set up chiffer groups, teaching a few select people coding and deciphering in his apartment. During the war he was responsible for the Norwegian Military Intelligence based in London.

An additional fun fact is that Roscher Lund's daughter, Vera Henriksen, grew up with chiffer groups in their home. She learned coding as a young child and became a XU agent by the age of sixteen. Later, she became an award-winning historical author and inspired me to want to write books.

Thank you for reading. I am so grateful for all your kind words. Don't miss out on the next book in this series.

To receive firsthand news about upcoming no-vels, please sign up for my newsletter here:

https://www.heidieljarbo.com/newsletter

PLEASE LEAVE A REVIEW

Thank you for reading *The Other Cipher*.
Reviews mean the world to an author. Please consider
leaving one for this book on your favorite store.
These reviews are greatly appreciated.

ABOUT THE AUTHOR

HEIDI ELJARBO grew up in a home filled with books and artwork, and she never truly imagined she would do anything other than write and paint. She studied art, languages, and history, all of which have come in handy when working as a freelance writer, magazine journalist, and painter.

After living in Canada, six US states, Japan, Switzerland, and Austria, Heidi now calls Norway home. She and her husband have a total of nine children, thirteen grandchildren—so far—in addition to a bouncy Wheaten Terrier.

The family's chosen retreat is a mountain cabin, where they hike in the summertime and ski the vast, white terrain during winter. Heidi's favorites are her family, God's beautiful nature, and the word *whimsical*.

If you would like to know more, please visit:

https://www.heidieljarbo.com/
https://www.instagram.com/heidieljarbo/?hl=nb
https://www.facebook.com/authorheidieljarbo/
https://no.pinterest.com/heidieljarbo/
Twitter: @HeidiEljarbo